RAZORBILL

Angel Kiss

Laura Jane Cassidy was born in 1986 in County Kildare
in Ireland and has taken time out from her Drama studies at
Trinity College Dublin to write full-time. She dislikes it when
people use the Internet to cheat at table quizzes, but likes it
when they use it to visit her popular blog, *laurajanecassidy.com*,
where she talks about book-related matters, as well as playlists,
fashion and lots of other stuff. *Angel Kiss* is her first novel.

LAURA JANE CASSIDY

Angel Kiss

razor
bill
PENGUIN

RAZORBILL

Published by the Penguin Group
Penguin Books Ltd, 80 Strand, London WC2R ORL, England
Penguin Group (USA) Inc., 375 Hudson Street, New York, New York 10014, USA
Penguin Group (Canada), 90 Eglinton Avenue East, Suite 700, Toronto, Ontario, Canada M4P 2Y3
(a division of Pearson Penguin Canada Inc.)
Penguin Ireland, 25 St Stephen's Green, Dublin 2, Ireland (a division of Penguin Books Ltd)
Penguin Group (Australia), 250 Camberwell Road, Camberwell, Victoria 3124, Australia
(a division of Pearson Australia Group Pty Ltd)
Penguin Books India Pvt Ltd, 11 Community Centre, Panchsheel Park, New Delhi – 110 017, India
Penguin Group (NZ), 67 Apollo Drive, Rosedale, Auckland 0632, New Zealand
(a division of Pearson New Zealand Ltd)
Penguin Books (South Africa) (Pty) Ltd, 24 Sturdee Avenue, Rosebank, Johannesburg 2196, South Africa

Penguin Books Ltd, Registered Offices: 80 Strand, London WC2R ORL, England

penguin.com

First published 2011
001 – 10 9 8 7 6 5 4 3 2 1

Set in 10.5/15.5 pt Sabon MT
Printed in Great Britain by Clays Ltd, St Ives plc

British Library Cataloguing in Publication Data
A CIP catalogue record for this book is available from the British Library

ISBN: 978-0-141-331775

www.greenpenguin.co.uk

MIX
Paper from
responsible sources
FSC™ C018179

Penguin Books is committed to a sustainable
future for our business, our readers and our
planet. This book is made from paper certified
by the Forest Stewardship Council.

To Jean, Joe and Liam,
with love.

Four
The number of wings on a wasp
The number of chambers in the heart
The number of strings on a violin
The number of photographs he gave me

Prologue

I sang and strummed over the whispered chatter of the crowded audience. Playing in this intimate Kilkenny club was a welcome break from the harsh tone of the Dublin circuit. I noticed a man coming in late, alone. He sat at the back but looked a little out of place; he was too neatly dressed, in a charcoal suit that matched his thinning hair. He held a large brown envelope in his left hand. I guessed who he was. In a way, I'd been expecting him.

When I'd finished my set he stood up and approached me. I slipped my guitar into its leather case and turned to face him.

'Jacki?'

I nodded. I could see his features clearly now. The edges of his brown eyes and his thin lips were creased with wrinkles.

'Can I speak to you outside?' he said.

I followed him to the smoking area outdoors where the cold night air hit me with force. The sky was studded with tiny sparkling stars. The centre of the courtyard was crowded with people huddling round gas heaters so we stood in a vacant corner. I was sorry I hadn't taken my coat out with me as goose bumps were appearing on my arms. My black lace dress was no barrier against the chill.

'My name is Detective Sergeant Matt Lawlor.' He held out his hand. The skin felt coarse, but his handshake was firm. 'I'm a member of a team working on Operation Trail, investigating the disappearance of a number of Irish women over the last ten years . . . We're concentrating on four cases at present.' He paused as if expecting a response. When all I offered was silence, he continued: 'I hoped you might be able to help, Jacki. Would you be prepared to help us?'

I'd guessed he was going to ask me this, but I couldn't answer straight away. I avoided his gaze and stared at the envelope in his hand. I wanted to help if I could . . . Well, help the victims and their families more than the police. But it was complicated. I felt completely torn. Last year hadn't been easy . . . I wasn't sure if I could go through it all again.

'I'll have to think about it,' I said. 'Can I get back to you?'

'Of course.' He held out the envelope. The top had been sealed with a strip of clear tape. I took it from him reluctantly.

'I'd appreciate it if you could give me a decision by the end of the week.'

He took a small white card from his inside pocket and gave it to me. His mobile number was scribbled on it in pencil. Just as I'd suspected, there was nothing official about our meeting.

That night I lay on the lumpy mattress of the hostel bed with the brown envelope hidden under my pillow. I tried to sleep but couldn't. Just before 3 a.m. I decided to tear the envelope open. Inside were four photographs. Four photographs of young women, each one prettier than the last. I felt my stomach knotting with tension.

Word had travelled from the Garda station in County Leitrim. Sergeant Lawlor had heard about my experiences in Avarna last summer. And now I had an important decision to make, but I didn't know if I could go through it all again.

Chapter 1

I watched the funeral pass by from the window of our cluttered caravan. The renovation of our new cottage was not yet complete, so that summer we were living in a little caravan at the top of our lane, overlooking the winding country road. My mum was among the cluster of darkly clad mourners headed to the graveyard. The body in the coffin was that of Jim Cullen. He was a popular man who had lived in a stone cottage about ten minutes' walk from the village of Avarna. Jim had died suddenly of a heart attack aged seventy-two. He was survived by his wife, Lily, and two children. I'd never met him.

We had been living there only two weeks. Mum had met him several times when she'd been house hunting in Avarna the previous year. It was Jim Cullen who had told her about one particular house that would be coming on the market, as its eccentric owner, a farrier named Alf, was moving to an island off the south coast. The moment she saw it Mum put in an offer and set about selling our house in Dublin. Thanks to the late Jim Cullen she had her idyllic country residence. I'd begged Mum not to accept the job, not to move. I really didn't want to live in the country. I'd screamed and cried and pleaded with her not to make me leave Dublin, but it was no use. She'd never understand just how hard it was for me to leave my friends, my school, my band, everything that was important to me.

When I protested about going to Jim's funeral she presumed it was because I was still mad at her. That was true, but there was another reason. I really disliked funerals. I'd always found myself sensitive to other people's suffering; I seemed to soak up their grief like a sponge. I already felt unwell that day; I had a headache and just knew I wouldn't be able to handle it. I watched until the large crowd passed and then went back to strumming my guitar.

Mum didn't go to the Cullen house for tea afterwards because she only vaguely knew Jim's relatives and didn't want to intrude. I noticed how her eyelids were red when she dozed off later. No doubt she felt just like me: the day's events had reminded her of my dad's funeral. He'd died of a brain tumour when I was nine and even after six years I could still recall the small details of that day. The navy woollen tights that made my legs itch, the smell of the white lilies laid out on the coffin and the grip of my mum's hand on my own small trembling one. He'd been sick for a while, but then suddenly he was gone and the funeral was the first time I began to accept this. Mum and I had learned to cope since then, but we still thought about him all the time. We liked to remember the happy times, how he'd always made us laugh . . . and the way he used to sing along really badly to the radio.

The caravan was a poor replacement for our suburban terraced house, but Mum had assured me that soon we would have a beautifully refurbished cottage, a home unblemished by memories, a fresh start. I missed Dublin so much that I couldn't really appreciate this. I was still coming to terms with the fact that I would have to move to a new school in September, make new friends, find a new band, basically rebuild all these vital parts of my life. I wasn't exactly looking forward to that. I was looking forward to moving into the house though. The caravan was unbelievably cramped, which didn't make things easy between me and Mum when we both needed our own space.

I'd thought living in a caravan would be great fun, kind of like living on a tour bus. And it had been fun . . . for about ten minutes. Mum had rented it online and somehow it looked massive in the images, but in reality it was more like one from an episode of *Father Ted* – except nobody was laughing when it was delivered and we saw how tiny it was. My head almost reached the roof, and I'm only five foot five. At one end there were two single couch beds with some very compact storage space underneath, and there was a table in between them that you could have either up or down. At the other end of the caravan there was a counter top with a hob and a kettle and two cupboards underneath. And in the middle, beside the tiny space that joined the 'bedroom and kitchen' (as the website had put it), was an even tinier bathroom. My bed was the most uncomfortable thing on the planet and I dreaded getting into it.

The night of Jim Cullen's funeral I slept uneasily and awoke from the strangest dream with the scene still vivid in my mind: a drunken man stumbled up a lane, struggling to stay upright. A car pulled up beside him, almost knocking him to the ground. The window rolled down. A hand emerged, clutching a brown leather handbag.

'*Here. Take this and burn it. Do you hear me? Burn it! This and everything in it.'* The hand was trembling but the voice was steady.

'Why the . . . why the hell should I?'

'Because if you don't I'll tell everyone what you did. Do you really want me to tell them about —'

'Fine . . . I'll burn the bloody bag. Whose is it anyway?'

He got no response. The car reversed out, leaving tyre marks in the earth. The drunken man continued up the dark lane, the bag dangling from his right hand.

Once was unsettling enough, but I'd had the same dream nearly every night that week. The way it was so clear in my mind was starting to scare me, and there was one particular thing about it that really freaked me out. I recognized the lane. It was the one that led to our new house. I didn't recognize the men though. I'd never seen them before and I certainly had no desire to. Particularly not the one sitting in the car. His pale eyes held a vicious manic stare that I couldn't forget.

As I tried to get back to sleep, the image of the bag kept coming into my mind. It was a satchel made of chocolate-brown leather, with a little handle as well as a longer strap, and it swung back and forth as the drunken man moved hesitantly along, the moonlight glinting off its gold buckles. The bag looked familiar, like something I'd see when I was searching through vintage shops for clothes.

I hate it when I'm trying to get back to sleep in the middle of the night and my mind won't stop racing. I tried hard to think about something else. Maybe I was so fixated on the dream because I didn't have anything more exciting to distract me. Clearly my anxiety over the move to Avarna had created a recurring nightmare composed of random memories. Once I felt settled I was sure it would go away. *I should spend more time exploring the village*, I thought. *I'm sure there were interesting little corners I hadn't yet discovered. Places like that café and the garden by the river, and that cute little clothes shop. It looked expensive but maybe I'd call in anyway . . .* Eventually, after the distraction of planning my tour of the village, my brain shut down and I fell into a welcome dream-free sleep.

The next morning there was a gorgeous blue sky and I felt a lot better. But we'd run out of milk so I couldn't have cereal. Instead of being annoyed I decided it was fate; I'd wander into the village to get some milk and explore a bit more.

As I walked into the local shop I heard a loud smack on the window. A fly swatter hit the windowpane with brutal force. I watched as the doomed wasp fell on to the dusty sill, its legs flickering for a moment before it died. The shop owner, Mary Reynolds, stood triumphantly, clasping the blue swatter.

'The little feckers come out earlier every year,' she said as she scooped the tiny corpse into a tissue and dumped it in the bin behind the counter. 'How are you, Jacki? Are you keeping well?'

'Yes, I'm fine, thanks,' I said, trying to be cheerful and heading for the fridge.

Mary knew all of Avarna's residents by name and there was little that happened in the village that she didn't find out about. The first time I'd gone into her shop was only for chewing gum, yet she'd kept me chatting for twenty minutes. She found out my name, my age, that my mum, Rachel, was the new primary school teacher starting in September, that I'd just done my Junior Cert. exams and that I didn't have a boyfriend. In return

I was subjected to her son Nick's entire life story. He was a year older than me, had just finished transition year, was allergic to tomatoes and played electric guitar.

Today I was spared from interrogation as she was soon chatting to another customer. She introduced me to Joe Clancy, owner of the aptly named Clancy's, one of Avarna's four pubs.

'And did you hear Tommy Ford's wife had a baby girl?' said Joe. 'I'm not sure what they called her . . .'

'Chloe Louise, eight pounds twelve ounces, big head of brown hair,' said Mary as she stared at the open window, daring another wasp to fly through it. The shop was uncomfortably warm, as was everywhere in the village during that unusually hot summer.

'Here's hoping she gets her looks from her mother,' said Joe. 'That fella Tommy has a face like a melted welly.'

'You're terrible,' said Mary with a laugh.

I smiled to myself. You couldn't help liking Mary, in spite of her knack for getting information out of everyone who came into the shop.

'Anyway, I better be off,' said Joe. He sauntered out with an ice-cream cone in his hand and a folded newspaper tucked under his elbow.

I checked the selection of biscuits, searching for my favourites.

'Nick!' shouted Mary. There was silence. 'Nick!' she bellowed again. A few moments later her son emerged from the store-room in the back with a copy of *Kerrang!* magazine in his hand and a disgruntled look on his face. Although I'd heard a lot about him from Mary, this was the first time I'd seen him. He was tall and slim and wore faded blue denims and a black T-shirt. His brown hair was quite long and curled across his forehead. As he came towards us I could see his striking blue eyes and that he had a few freckles on his cheeks. His arms were strong and tanned.

One syllable echoed silently inside my head: Wow. Nick was gorgeous, even with that grumpy look on his face.

'Nick, I have to go to the wholesaler's, so stay behind the counter, will you?' said Mary. She mustn't have realized we hadn't been introduced.

Nick nodded grudgingly and slumped down on the stool behind the till.

'Bye, Jacki,' said Mary, and then she hurried out the door, taking with her any affection I felt for my ex-boyfriend in Dublin. I took out my purse and approached the counter with my milk and biscuits.

'Hi,' he said.

'Hi.'

I tried to think of something intelligent to say, but failed miserably.

'That's two ninety-five,' said Nick.

'Thanks,' I murmured as I handed him three euro with a slightly shaking hand.

'So, you're Jacki?' he asked as his eyes met mine, and he dropped the change into my palm. My insides jolted when I heard him say my name.

'Eh . . . yeah. You must be Nick.' There were a few moments of silence. I tried to think of something to say. Anything at all. But nothing came.

'So how are you finding Avarna so far?'

'Yeah it's . . . it's cool.' Avarna was a lot of things, but cool certainly was not one of them. Why did I have to say cool? Any other word would have done. Any one at all.

'That's good,' said Nick. He smiled at me. I could feel my cheeks warming. The thought that they were undoubtedly bright red made me cringe.

'OK, I better be off,' I said. I wanted to get out of there before I said something else embarrassing.

'See you around,' he said.

And then it came. Whatever possessed me to wave at someone whose handsome face was a mere metre away from me I will never know. But I did. I gave him a big giant wave. He looked at me a little strangely as I turned away, embarrassed, and rushed out of the shop, my cheeks burning so brightly I could almost feel my new social life going up in flames.

Chapter 2

The next morning I got up early. I put on my purple skinny jeans and Led Zeppelin T-shirt, ran my fingers through my hair and swept some black mascara on to my eyelashes. I slipped a couple of bracelets on my wrist and checked my reflection in the mirror before heading outside. Work on the site had stopped as the builders were having their morning tea break. Mum was standing beside the empty cement mixer talking to Des, our electrician. She was nearly forty but could easily have passed for younger in her cream top and denims, and with straight blonde hair like mine that rested just above her shoulders. I had a feeling from the way he'd been hanging around lately that Des fancied my mum, but there was no way that was going to happen. She hadn't so much as looked at another man since my dad died. The sooner Des realized that and stopped trying to flirt with her the better. As I walked towards them, avoiding the muddy areas and the builders' mess, I caught some of their conversation.

'Did you get your hair done, Rachel?' said Des.

'Just a trim,' said Mum. 'Can't believe you noticed.'

How creepy, I thought. Poor Mum, she was way too polite for her own good.

'It's very nice . . . very . . . shiny,' said Des with an elaborate hand movement that I presumed was supposed to convey shine. Then he went slightly red and started to mumble something under his breath. Unable to watch his cringeworthy antics any longer, I turned and headed for the road, saying I was just going to get something from the shop. We were running low on bread, but I was really just hoping to see Nick again.

As I wandered towards the village, I thought about how it can take seconds to create an obsession, and years to get over it. Within minutes of meeting Nick I'd allowed myself to slip into that familiarly dangerous territory. That place where you think about a person constantly, where you rehearse future conversations in your head, where you plan your day around the blissful possibility of bumping into them. I'd only been in love once before. It had ended when I'd discovered my now ex-boyfriend, Cian, wrapped round my former best friend.

I still wasn't used to walking on the country roads but I loved picking the tall grass and the wildflowers along the way. Mum had told me to walk facing the oncoming traffic so I could be seen, but sometimes it felt like I was staring straight into certain death. I nearly stepped right into the ditch whenever I heard a car coming.

I plucked the petals off a yellow flower as I walked along, thinking about how you put everything into your first love, because you really believe it's going to last forever. That is its triumph and its tragedy, the reason you will never forget it, and the reason it is so difficult to let go. I'd spent my first couple of weeks in Avarna missing Cian in spite of everything that had happened. But then along came Nick. He was handsome and charming and loved music. Basically, he was perfect.

When I arrived at the shop I caught a glimpse of Nick through the window and felt a flutter of excitement. He was wearing a white T-shirt and was talking to a customer. The door made a little *ding* as I pushed it open. A girl was standing in front of the counter talking to him, her long black hair scraped back from her pretty face.

'Hi, Nick,' I said, trying to sound as casual as possible.

'Hi, Jacki.' He turned back to the girl and smiled. 'Sarah, this is Jacki, the girl I was telling you about.'

My heart almost stopped beating. He'd been talking about me?

'Jacki, this is my girlfriend, Sarah.'

This time my heart almost stopped beating again, but for an entirely different reason. *My girlfriend*. It's amazing how a mere two words can change the mood of an entire day. How could I not have presumed it anyway? He's such a good-looking guy . . . of course he would be taken. And he seemed so proud as he said it: *my girlfriend*. He was clearly happy with her. Sarah appeared friendly, although her eager smile seemed a little fake. As we made polite conversation I got the impression she would rather I wasn't there. My new life went crashing back to boring. I quickly bought some bread and made my escape.

Head down, ego deflated, I reached the bottom of our lane.

'Jacki! Will you check if there's any post?' Mum called from the caravan door. I struggled to find the rusty red postbox hidden among the overgrown bushes. There was no key for it, so I got a stick to prise the letters out. At first I thought it was empty, but then I felt the stick touch some paper at the very bottom. I couldn't get it out: it was firmly stuck inside. I was going to just leave it there, but that little voice in your head that speaks to you when you least expect it told me to try harder. I forced my hand in through the opening, and gripped the letter with my fingers. For one horrible moment I thought my arm might be stuck. I yanked it out, managing to scrape some skin off the back of my hand. But I soon forgot about my stinging skin when I saw the letter.

It was addressed in neat writing to a Mr Alf Meehan. The ink was faded and the stamp foreign and it was dated about six months earlier. I should have given it to someone to forward to him, but that persuasive inner voice suggested that I open it. Before I knew what I was doing the envelope was open in my hands. I pulled out a slip of cream notepaper. Unfolding it, I felt a shiver run through me as I read the bold black letters:

KEEP YOUR MOUTH SHUT

I spent most of the afternoon lounging in the caravan. I didn't really feel up to doing anything else.

'What's wrong with you, Jacki?' Mum asked.

'What do you mean?' I said, looking away from the window.

Mum was sitting cross-legged on her bed, flicking through a home-decorating magazine.

'You've been moping around all afternoon,' she said.

'No, I haven't.'

'Yes, you have.'

'Well, sorry.' I'd gone for a short walk after lunch just to try to clear my head and cheer myself up, but obviously that hadn't worked very well. I'd come back feeling more down than ever. Ever since I'd opened the envelope I'd felt very sick. The threatening note had freaked me out slightly. I needed to forget about it: it had nothing to do with me.

I grabbed my phone off the ledge beside the bed and sighed when I saw that I still had no coverage. I hated that it was nearly impossible to get even one bar of coverage up here. Not to mention the fact that we didn't have any Internet. I hadn't been online in days. There was broadband available in the café in the village, but it had been closed for the past week. My life was a total mess. All my friends were in Dublin. I couldn't even ring them, for heaven's sake. I missed them and I missed my computer, I missed playing music, I missed everything. And the first guy I'd fancied in months, and who I'd got my hopes stupidly high about, had a girlfriend. A gorgeous girlfriend called Sarah.

A few minutes later I glanced at my phone again, and could hardly believe it when I saw one teeny bar. Yay! Contact with the real world. Afraid to move the phone, I lay down on the bed and dialled my friend Hannah's number. It rang and rang.

I decided to text Ross rather than ring him, because I knew he'd be in work. I wrote a text that spanned three messages, ranting about how boring Avarna was and how much I missed Dublin. In his signature goofy tone he replied, 'Keep calm and rock on.' Great. Thanks, Ross.

I called Sophie too, but it also rang without answer and I got a text from her a few minutes later saying that she was jamming with her brother's band and that she'd call me after-wards. I got a horrible sinking feeling. I hadn't talked to her in days – she could at least have spoken to me for two minutes. I tried not to get mad though. It wasn't her fault Mum had made me move to the middle of nowhere.

I picked up a marker and started to doodle on my hand. I liked drawing little sketches on my skin – plans for the tattoo

I was going to get once Mum finally gave in and let me. Earlier I'd drawn a heart, broken down the middle, on the inside of my right wrist, where I hoped to eventually get a treble clef tattooed. Mum sat down beside me and gave me a gentle squeeze.

'Your heart's not broken. It's still in one piece,' she said, pulling my hair back from my neck and prodding the little heart-shaped freckle below my left ear. I couldn't resist smiling too. It was in the perfect shape of a heart, tiny but distinct. My gran had been the first one to notice it, and had always insisted that I'd been kissed by an angel.

I smiled at Mum. No matter how much I hated it that she'd dragged me here, I still couldn't help loving her more than anyone else in the world. Since it had been just us we'd grown closer than any other mother and daughter I knew. We screamed and shouted and fought and bickered, but we adored each other all the same.

Apart from hating the thought of a treble-clef tattoo, Mum had always been supportive of my love for music. She'd spent her entire childhood dreaming of being a movie star. She'd had half a dozen posters of Marilyn Monroe taped to her wall and had watched *Some Like It Hot* hundreds of times. But my grandparents insisted that acting was just a hobby, and that she couldn't possibly expect to pursue it as a career. So from the time I was four and had said I wanted to be a rock star, Mum had been driving me to guitar lessons, saving up for music equipment and listening to me singing much too loudly around the house. Her only request was that if I became famous I would dedicate one of my songs to her. I decided that was a fair trade.

I waited until she'd left the caravan, then took Alf Meehan's letter out from my back pocket. I knelt down on the floor beside my bed and pulled out my suitcase. Mum had allowed me to bring just one suitcase of stuff to the caravan, as there wasn't room for any more. It was packed full of clothes and a Converse shoebox that held my most prized possessions including a little silver bracelet given to me by my dad, my purple hardback notebook that I wrote my lyrics in, a couple of photographs of my friends and me and a battered paperback copy of *The Commitments*. I carefully hid the letter in the shoebox and placed it back in the suitcase. I knew Mum wouldn't be impressed that I'd opened someone else's post. I didn't even know why I had, so there was no way I'd be able to explain it to her. But something was stopping me from throwing it away.

When I stepped out of the caravan Des was talking to Mum again. I decided to go over and rescue her. But the closer I got to them the more freaked out I became. Mum was standing close to Des and twirling a strand of her hair. Then I heard her giggle. This was actually making me queasy. I wanted to turn round and go back but Des had spotted me.

'Jacki, we were just talking about you . . .'

I faked a smile and walked towards them.

'Hi,' I said to Des. A *hi* that said *If you lay one finger on my mother, I will most certainly strangle you*. He didn't seem to notice.

'So,' he said, 'your mum was telling me you like to play guitar? And that you're in a band?'

'*Was* in a band,' I corrected him. 'I had to leave it because we were moving here.' Myself, Sophie and Ross had played together, but we'd all agreed that there was no way we could keep it up now that I was living so far away. I'd also done a stint in my cousin Steve's heavy metal band. I wasn't majorly into heavy metal, but they were all eighteen and I got to play in Whelan's a few times. The bouncers got to know me, and so Hannah and I had managed to get into a couple of other gigs there on Saturday nights. It's amazing where a fake ID, a push-up bra and a familiar face can get you.

'And you like Thin Lizzy?' said Des.

'Love them,' I said.

'I went to see them in Slane in eighty-one,' he said. 'Best gig of my life.'

'Wow, legend,' I said limply.

OK, so Des was going up in my estimation. But only slightly.

'Oh, by the way, Jacki,' said Mum. 'You and I are going to the Smyths' house for dinner in half an hour.'

'Where?' I asked.

'The Smyths. They own the guesthouse on the main street. I met Brigid in the shop and she invited us down. It was so thoughtful of her – she said I must be tired of trying to cook in the caravan.'

I'd never met any of the Smyths but I'd seen the guesthouse where they lived. It was across from Mary's shop and painted an insanely bright yellow.

'Do you know the Smyths well, Des?' said Mum.

'Ah yeah, Brigid and Pa are lovely people. They have a son your age, Jacki. And I'm good friends with Brigid's sister, Lydia. She lives there with them too. She's a dressmaker.'

So they had a son my age, did they? My mood lifted a little bit. I looked down at my jeans and T-shirt and made an excuse to get back to the caravan. Now that it seemed Cian and Nick were in the past, maybe I needed to dress for the future.

Chapter 3

The Smyths' sitting room resembled the chaotic interior of a back-street antique store. I breathed in the stuffy air as I sat on the couch among the tasselled cushions, staring up at the dusty chandelier. I like antique stores. I like rummaging through all the objects to find hidden treasures. In that sitting room I longed to examine the ornaments and the photographs and memorabilia, but I couldn't, because Colin Smyth sat on the chair across from me, his eyes fixed on the flickering television. He had a thick mop of red hair and his attractive face was covered in pale freckles. He wore a blue shirt and grey cord trousers.

Quite a stylish dresser, I thought. Back in the caravan I'd frantically tried to make myself look presentable. I was wearing a short purple velvet dress that I'd bought in a vintage shop, black fishnet tights and black Converse. Although Colin wasn't really my type, he had a certain cuteness, so I was glad I'd made an effort.

Colin hadn't said much during dinner but he seemed nice. He had happily obliged when Brigid suggested that he bring me into the sitting room to watch TV, but he totally avoided making eye contact with me. I don't normally like people who do this – it makes me uneasy. But I decided to let Colin off the hook, as he just seemed to be a bit shy.

We hadn't spoken a word since we sat down in front of the TV. I tried to think of a conversation starter as I scanned the framed paintings and prints that clashed with the floral-papered walls.

Several times it seemed as if Colin was about to say something, but then he would just look back at the television, pretending to be enthralled by it. Then when he wasn't flicking through the channels he was fidgeting with the button on his shirtsleeve. He twisted it round and round and round.

Just think of something to say, Jacki. Anything at all.

Round and round it twirled, then – *ping!* – the button bounced on to the wooden floor and rolled away, skimming the rug and disappearing from view. Colin's face went bright red. I stood up to look for it.

'It's OK. It doesn't matt—'

'I think it went over here,' I said.

I knelt down to check under a glass-fronted cabinet, but was distracted by the unusual objects inside. These included a perfume bottle, a magnifying glass and a delicately painted porcelain egg with a hinge on the side. I very much wanted to open the egg to see what was in it.

'Found it!' said Colin.

'Thought you two might like a snack –' Brigid Smyth walked in with a bowl of freshly made popcorn to find us both on our knees on the floor.

'Oh . . . thanks,' I said, scrambling back to the couch.

'Are you two OK?'

'Yes, Mam,' said Colin. 'We were just looking for my button.' He held it up to show her.

'Oh, right,' she said. 'I'll leave you to it then.' She headed back to the kitchen.

Colin took a handful of popcorn from the bowl. I noticed that there were flecks of paint on the backs of his hands and remembered Brigid had said at dinner that Colin liked art, so I decided to spark up a conversation and find out more.

'What kind of art do you do?' I said. I liked drawing, but I wasn't very good at art and I didn't know a lot about it.

'Oh, I like lots of different styles. At the moment I'm really into Manga-inspired stuff, you know, like the Japanese comics,' he answered, shifting his gaze away from the TV and looking at me instead.

'Wow, that sounds really cool.' My friend Hannah would've been disgusted if she'd heard me say that. Last year her brother had done a twenty-four-hour comic workshop in Dublin with some famous Manga artist. She said she wouldn't be seen dead going to such a nerdfest. But Hannah wasn't here now, and I really needed to make some new friends.

'Yeah, I read a lot of Manga,' said Colin, 'so I like drawing that sort of stuff. Anything Japanese really fascinates me.'

'How do you do it?' I asked. 'Do you use a computer?'

'First I make a sketch,' he said, sitting up a little bit straighter, 'then scan it on to my laptop. Then I either work on it digitally, or print it off and use ink and watercolours. That's what I was doing today, before dinner. I just finished one off.' It seemed that Colin could be quite talkative once he was concentrating on a topic that interested him.

'Can I see it?' I said.

He hesitated for a moment but then got up from his armchair and lowered the brass handles of the doors that separated us from the next room. Then he pushed them open to reveal possibly the coolest bedroom I've ever seen.

'This is your room?' I said in awe.

'Yep,' said Colin, clearing a path through the chaos of clothes and comics on the floor. 'One summer Mam wanted to use my old bedroom for some guests so I got shoved in here. I really like it so I convinced her to let me keep it.'

Colin's bedroom was really big, just slightly smaller than the sitting room. The walls were covered in various Japanese film posters. I recognized *Akira* and *Spirited Away*. Computer games and DVDs were stacked beside a TV along with an assortment of anime figures. There were a couple of plates and glasses on the floor. The blue duvet cover was crumpled up at the foot of the bed and a noticeboard hung over the headboard with tons of stuff pinned to it – sketches, magazine clippings, ticket stubs. The computer desk was littered with pens, pencils and discarded pieces of paper. I followed Colin through the mess to the back corner of the room. A wooden easel stood there, holding a recently completed project. It was of a girl with jet-black hair and blood-red lips. Her head was bowed and a single red tear, like a drop of blood, stained her white cheek. The overall effect was striking, and I was captivated by it.

'It's incredible,' I said. 'You're really talented.'

I couldn't take my eyes off it.

'Thanks,' he said, blushing slightly.

'Is she based on anyone you know?' I asked, as I took in all the detail.

'No, she just sort of appeared in my head.'

I knew what Colin meant. Sometimes ideas for songs just popped into my head, and I had no idea where they came from.

'Are you going to do art in college?' I asked, still fascinated by his painting.

'Hopefully,' said Colin, flopping down on the swivel chair at his desk. 'I'd really like to study in New York. What do you want to do in college?' He had this intense look when he asked questions, like he was really interested in what I had to say. His initial shyness seemed to have vanished, and I felt relaxed in his company.

'Music, I suppose. All I really want to do is sing and play guitar. But I've got another three years before I have to think about college. I was actually hoping to work on a demo this year . . .'

I surprised myself by telling him that. Maybe Colin would turn out to be one of those people you could share your secrets with. I was even beginning to wonder if I could fancy him.

'I can't wait to finish school,' he said. 'It's so boring sometimes. Anyway, wanna go back and watch TV?'

I couldn't help looking longingly at his computer. I was having serious withdrawal symptoms.

'Em . . . would you mind if I used your computer for a few minutes? We don't have Internet in the caravan and I'd love to just check my messages . . .'

'Sure. Knock yourself out,' he said, pushing some rubbish off the keyboard.

I sat at his desk and logged on while Colin lay down on his bed and picked up a book.

Fifteen messages. The first was from Hannah wondering how I was. The next five were Hannah wondering why I hadn't messaged her back. She wanted to know was I mad at her because she kissed Ross? Hannah and Ross. Weird. I wasn't mad though. I used to fancy him, but then I'd seen him throw up after drinking too much cider, and the attraction had dwindled. I presumed they wouldn't last very long anyway. Hannah disposed of boys just as often as she blew her allowance on Topshop accessories, i.e. almost every fortnight. The next message was a dirty joke forwarded by Ross to me and twenty other people. And the next was a picture of a tiny kitten wearing a top hat, forwarded by Sophie. The rest were spam. I quickly replied to Hannah, explaining why I hadn't been in contact.

'Thanks, Colin,' I said when I'd logged out. 'I really miss having Internet; you feel so cut off without it. I can get it on my phone but I never have enough credit and the coverage is really bad here anyway so it takes forever to load.'

'Tell me about it – it's so annoying. You're welcome to come down here and use it any time you want,' he said.

'Oh, thanks!'

Colin was turning out to be a nice guy.

'I'm sure you could even stay over sometime if you needed a break. I'd go insane if I had to live in the same room as my mam.'

'Wouldn't your mam have something to say about . . . y'know, me staying here?'

'Nah, she wouldn't mind, she knows you're not my type,' said Colin with a laugh.

'Well, you're not my type either!' I snapped.

'No, sorry, that's not what I meant, Jacki. I'm . . . I'm gay. Sorry, I presumed you knew.' Colin looked down at his feet, and I instantly regretted being so snappy.

He'd taken me completely by surprise. 'Oh! No . . . nobody told me.'

'Well, it's not such a big deal any more, I suppose. It was hard at first, but I came out last year so by now most people around here just accept it.'

'That's really cool. And I would definitely like to stay over sometime.'

'So what's *your* type then?' said Colin as I followed him back into the sitting room.

'Em . . . I dunno really,' I said, but Nick Reynolds's name suddenly popped into my head. I had tried to forget about him, but I just wasn't able to. Colin probably knew him . . . It was such a small village. Maybe I could find out more about him. 'So . . .' I said. 'I was thinking maybe you could introduce me to some of your friends? I know literally nobody here.'

'Sure, there's a good gang in Avarna. I'll let you know what's going on. Here, let me take your number now,' he said, taking out his phone.

'Thanks,' I said with a smile and called it out. 'Well . . . I've already met two people: Nick from the shop and his girlfriend, but only briefly.'

'Nick's one of my best mates!' said Colin excitedly.

'No way.' I tried to sound casual, but was really happy to hear that. I thought of quizzing Colin about Nick and Sarah's relationship, but I didn't want to be too obvious, so I decided to leave it till another time.

Through the sitting-room window I could see Des's van pulling up outside his terraced house across the road. He walked round the van and helped an old woman out of the passenger side. Taking her by the arm, he led her to his front door.

'Is that Des's mum?' I asked.

Colin glanced out the window. 'Yes. He lives with her. She hasn't been too well lately.'

'What's wrong with her?'

'She had pneumonia.'

'Oh no, the poor woman.' I watched the dark figures moving behind the lace curtains.

'She's recovering though,' said Colin, leaning back on the couch.

'Did his wife die? Or is he divorced?' I asked as I rearranged the cushions a bit to get comfortable.

'He never married,' said Colin.

'Really?' I decided not to mention Des and my mum. Talking about something can make it feel more real sometimes. And there was no way I wanted him to become part of our lives.

Just as Des's door closed, the door of the shop opened and Mary walked out and got into her car.

'Have you met the infamous Mary Reynolds yet?' said Colin, nodding in her direction.

'I have indeed.'

'Very quiet woman,' he said. I giggled. 'Mary's one of my aunt Lydia's best friends,' he added, offering me some more popcorn. 'She and my mam are organizing a surprise fiftieth for Mary. Along with Joe Clancy.'

'Oh, your mam was telling us about that earlier. I'd say Mary will be delighted.'

'It should be good craic.'

I finished off my handful of popcorn, then looked over at the cabinet again.

'Where did you get that?' I asked, pointing at the porcelain egg.

'The egg? Oh, it's Lydia's. It's been there for years. Why?'

'No reason really. I just think it's really pretty. I used to have one with a little swan inside it. My dad bought it for me. But I broke it.' I'd dropped it a few weeks before he died and had been really upset because I loved it. He'd promised to buy me a new one, but he never got the chance.

'Where is your dad tonight?' asked Colin.

'My dad . . . he died a few years ago,' I said.

'I didn't realize . . . sorry.' Colin started to fidget with his sleeve again.

'It's OK,' I said. 'You couldn't have known. He died when I was nine.' Sometimes it surprised me how easily I was able to talk about my dad now.

'What happened to him?' asked Colin.

'He had a tumour. He'd been sick for a while.'

Colin nodded and then looked away.

'Is there something inside that one?' I said, changing the subject.

'Which?'

'The egg; is there something inside it?' I'm not sure why, but I really wanted to touch it. Maybe because it brought back memories.

'Open it if you want.'

'Can I?' I didn't know why I felt such a rush of excitement.

'Yeah, sure.'

I opened the door of the wooden cabinet, clasped my fingers round the smooth turquoise porcelain and lifted the egg out. I gently pulled it open. Inside there was a little silver heart, studded with tiny sparkling crystals.

'Wow.'

'Nice, isn't it?' said Colin. 'I used to be fascinated by it as a kid. But I wasn't allowed to touch it. I used to open it when Lydia wasn't here. She'd have killed me if she'd found out.'

I stared at it for a few moments. As I placed it back in the cabinet I could hear loud music blasting through the wall.

'Is that Iggy Pop?'

'Yep.'

'Where is it coming from?'

'Lydia's shop,' said Colin. 'She's a little bit crazy, in a good way. Come on and I'll introduce you.'

I followed Colin out the front door. Just a few steps away was the bright shopfront of Lydia Jones Designs. I'd spotted it on our first visit to the village, but figured it would be way too expensive for my budget. Colin pushed open the door and we stepped into a wonderful little clothes store. Racks of beautiful handmade dresses hung on multicoloured beaded hangers, and pink shelves held suede clutch bags and charming costume jewellery. A half mannequin in the centre wore a pretty red dress with an empire waist and lace hem.

Colin weaved through the racks towards the back of the shop where a woman whom I guessed was Lydia sat at a desk working on a sewing machine. She was surrounded by a mess of fabric and buttons and beads, and clearly hadn't heard us come in. She was bopping her head up and down, and singing along to the music. Like Colin she had pale skin, but hers had only a few freckles. Her hair was dyed purple and she wore what looked like one of her own designs, a yellow shift dress with a collar of white felt daisies. It was the kind of outfit that only somebody very quirky could pull off.

Colin waved his hand in front of her face and her head jerked up. She reached for the stereo and turned the music down.

'Hello!' she said in a cheery voice.

'This is Jacki,' said Colin. 'She's just moved here.'

'Hi, Jacki, nice to meet you.' She stood up and held out her hand. I noticed that her fingernails were painted neon pink.

'Nice to meet you too,' I said, shaking her hand. 'I really like your dresses. They're amazing.'

'And your dress is adorable,' she said.

'Oh, thanks!'

'I love vintage too. I use a lot of antique materials in my designs.' Lydia sat back down on her swivel chair.

'People come from all over to get dresses made here,' said Colin. 'She's practically famous.'

'Oh, stop!' said Lydia with a giggle.

I liked Lydia immediately. She was wonderfully weird.

'We could hear your music through the wall again,' said Colin, picking up a piece of blue fabric from one of the chairs and fashioning it into a belt round his waist.

'I can't concentrate without loud music,' Lydia explained. 'I need it, but it drives my sister crazy.'

'You need to get earphones,' said Colin.

'It's not the same,' said Lydia and I in unison, and we both laughed. 'I play albums on repeat when I'm working on a design,' Lydia added. 'Each dress a different album. *Lust for Life* will forever be fused in my brain with metal sequins and lace.'

Colin was so lucky – I would have loved an aunt like Lydia. I couldn't imagine her being best friends with Mary though. The two of them were completely different.

'Anyway, what do you guys think?' Lydia held up the dress. It was beautiful, turquoise with a purple lace hem and metal sequins on the bodice.

'Wow. That's the prettiest dress I've ever seen,' I said.

'Fabulous!' said Colin.

'It's the same colour as your porcelain egg,' I noticed.

'Yes, it's exactly the same colour,' said Colin. 'Where did you get that egg again?'

'What egg?' Lydia enquired, fixing the dress's collar.

'The porcelain egg in the cabinet. Jacki was admiring it.'

'Oh, that thing. A friend gave it to me. A long time ago.'

'Which friend was that?' asked Colin.

'Just an old friend – you don't know her.'

'It's lovely,' I said.

Lydia looked thoughtful for a moment. 'Yes, it is nice,' she agreed.

'Colin, are you in there?' called Brigid from the doorway. 'Jacki's mum is heading home.'

'I'd better go,' I said. 'I'll be back to have a look around your shop sometime.'

'Yes, definitely drop in,' said Lydia. 'We can listen to extra-loud music together.'

Colin walked me out to the shop door and even gave me a hug as we said our goodbyes.

I lay in bed that night smiling, pleased that I'd actually made a new friend. Colin was so cool and, as an added bonus, he knew Nick really well. I realized Nick had a girlfriend, but maybe they hadn't been going out that long. Or maybe they'd been going out for ages and were headed for a break-up. A girl can dream.

Chapter 4

The following afternoon I sat on my bed, reading Mum's copy of *Vogue*. I was flicking absent-mindedly through the pages when I came across an article called 'Interpreting Your Dreams'. I sat up a little straighter, excited that I might finally get some insight into my one. I scanned through it and, sure enough, there was a bit about recurring nightmares.

'*These dreams are probably trying to tell you something. Dreams like these are often chilling and frightening, which makes you take notice of them.*'

So my dream was trying to tell me something. What the hell was it trying to say?

'Read my horoscope!' said Mum, having spotted me with the magazine. She stirred her coffee and sat down at the table.

'Mum, you know I think horoscopes are a load of rubbish,' I reminded her.

'Read it anyway – it's a bit of fun. Go on . . .' she said, poking me on the shoulder.

'Fine.' I put on my best mystical voice. '*Love is on the horizon, and a long-term union may materialize in the near future. A certain someone could revolutionize important aspects of your life.*'

Mum smiled to herself and I rolled my eyes.

'I'll read yours,' she said, snatching the magazine before I could object. '*A testing time awaits you. Events force you to examine your fundamental beliefs and to question your path in life.* How dramatic! A testing time awaits you, Jacki!'

'Yeah, me and all the other Capricorns on the planet.'

'You're so sceptical,' said Mum in exasperation.

'I don't see a problem with that,' I said, adjusting my pillow. 'Have you got any other magazines?'

'No. But I do have this.' She threw a copy of the local newspaper on to my lap.

I flicked through the pages, spotting some people I recognized from the village in the 'Out and about' section. There were photos from an eighteenth birthday party, and it looked like the birthday girl had been snapped mid-sentence, because her face was weirdly scrunched up. It reminded me of the photo of Hannah and me that Sophie had put online a few months ago. We'd been laughing at something, and hadn't realized there was a camera around. As a result we both looked deranged and very unattractive. Sophie was terrible for not censoring her photos and just putting anything up. At least the paper would be in everyone's recycling bin next week but those photos were online forever. There were a few planning notices at the back of the paper and then a list of anniversaries. My eyes were drawn to the last one.

CULLEN – *Birthday remembrance of our dear daughter Beth Cullen, late of Miner's Way, Avarna, whose birthday occurs on 16 July. Always remembered by your loving family.*

I wondered if she was related to Jim Cullen, the man who'd just died. Avarna was a small village so it was possible. The notice didn't say when the daughter had died but if it was the same family then they'd been through a double tragedy.

Later that evening, Mum put on her long grey cardigan and stepped into her pink wellingtons. 'I'm just going out to the house for a minute,' she said.

'I'll come with you,' I offered.

Mum took the torch with her as the evening light was fading and the electricity wasn't connected in the house. I closed the caravan door and followed Mum up the front garden. When we'd first visited the house, the garden had been my favourite part. The house had been shabby and rundown but the garden was overgrown and beautiful. It was full of wild flowers and reminded me of the gardens in Jane Austen adaptations that my mum and I used to watch on TV when I was little. Right now it was in a bit of a mess because of all the work that was going on, but the house was coming along nicely. The new windows and doors had been fitted, the gable had been painted and the broken roof tiles had been replaced. I couldn't wait until everything was finished and we could move in. I had convinced myself that once we moved into the house my recurring nightmare would stop and things would start to fall into place. At the moment we were in a kind of limbo. The caravan was a capsule, suspending us between our old life and our new one.

There was a quarter of an acre of barren ground at the rear of the house, surrounded by a rotting wooden fence and an overgrown hedge. It was full of building materials and rubbish and I tried to imagine it with nice paving and potted plants. On a bright day you could see the beautiful mountains in the distance and I was sure it would be a nice place to sit once it was cleaned up.

We went in through the back door. Mum tidied up some plates and cutlery that the builders had left. The kitchen units had all been ripped out and the space they once occupied was now a blank grey canvas. The linoleum had been taken away and the wooden floorboards were being restored to their original glory. Mum was excited about our new kitchen arriving in a couple of days.

'Jacki,' she said, 'remember you have to pick out a colour for your room.'

'I think I'll go for purple,' I said as we stood in the centre of my new bedroom with Mum shining the torch against the bare wall in front of us. As an only child I was used to having space to myself, but this was amazing. Or maybe it seemed huge because it was completely empty. I began to imagine where my bed would go. I'd definitely like it to face the bay window that looked out on to the front garden.

My new room had been Alf's old living room and a marble fireplace still stood against one wall.

'I thought it would be a shame to rip this out. Maybe you could keep it, put candles in it or something,' said Mum, resting her hand on one of the cream marble corners. 'It's obviously as old as the house, but strange . . . it looks almost new.' Mum was right. Like everything else in this house the fireplace was covered in dirt and dust from a lifetime of neglect. It was clear that housework had not been one of Alf's priorities. But this fireplace looked like it had never been used.

'Yes,' I said. 'I'll keep it.'

I loved my new room. I'd already bought some stuff for it, including a multicoloured plastic chandelier, a zebra-print noticeboard and a black and white framed photo of Bob Dylan. The chandelier lay in the corner, waiting to be installed. And I'd need to get a big wardrobe for all my clothes. I looked around the room trying to decide where that would go . . . One of my favourite pastimes was rooting through charity shops, so I'd accumulated a lot of stuff over the years. I loved owning stuff that other people didn't have, instead of just buying everything in the high street. Of course I loved shopping there too – I didn't say no to any kind of shopping! But I always found such great stuff in unexpected places. My top five finds so far had been a rare Thin Lizzy T-shirt, an old typewriter that someone had painted pink, an 80s tartan miniskirt, a vintage microphone and a gorgeous black lace dress. You had to root around to find the really good stuff, so I was proud of my unearthed treasures.

Mum walked around the room, smiling. Unlike me, she was particularly excited about her new life, her fresh start. Dad's death had been very hard for her. Up until last Christmas all of my dad's clothes had still hung in his half of the wardrobe, untouched for six years. Then one night Mum bundled them all into black plastic bags. They lay at the foot of her bed for three days before she carried them out to the car and took them to a charity shop on the other side of the city. I was sort of glad to see them go. I knew Mum still loved my dad very much, but I didn't think it was healthy to be living in a bedroom with all his stuff untouched, as if he was going to walk in and climb into bed any second. He was never going to do that. It was heartbreaking. But it was true.

'Wait till Des sees this!' said Mum, lifting up the chandelier so that it dangled in front of our faces. 'He'll think we've gone mad.'

I ran my fingers across the plastic droplets of the chandelier, collecting grey dust on my fingertip.

I tried to smile, and then walked back towards the door so she wouldn't see the tears in my eyes. Excited as I was about the new house, moving on was clearly going to be more painful than I'd anticipated.

When I woke up the next morning I felt as if I had scalded the inside of my skull. My head throbbed horribly from the moment I opened my eyelids and saw the cream ceiling of the caravan. But I was glad to be awake when being asleep these days meant having to endure the strange nightmare. I scrunched up my eyes and fiercely massaged the bridge of my nose. It felt like a tight rubber band was digging into the sides of my skull and at intervals someone was pulling it back and letting it snap against my temples.

When I shut my eyes, fragmented scenes from my nightmare would spin about in front of me, my mind twisting in a kaleidoscopic chaos. I would experience the anger and fear of those two men. I would see every single detail. The previous night I was so close to that brown bag that I could almost smell the leather and could see the cracks underneath the buckle. It felt like the man in the car was shouting directly into my ear and I could feel his breath against my cheek. *'Take this and burn it. Do you hear me? Burn it!'* I shuddered as I remembered.

The pain in my head wouldn't go away so I made my way over to the sink, poured a glass of water and took two painkillers.

The sun wasn't shining like it had on previous days but it was still very warm: I could feel humid air come in through the open window. The backs of my eyes burned as I rested my forehead in my hands and waited.

'What's wrong with you?' asked Mum as she came back inside, carrying cards of paint samples.

'I have a headache,' I muttered. It was out of my mouth before I had time to think, and Mum had grabbed her phone and gone out the door before I'd even looked up. I knew that as soon as she'd walked far enough to get coverage, she'd call the doctor. You didn't say the word 'headache' to Mum. Because my dad had died of a brain tumour, she insisted that you couldn't be too careful when it came to investigating any sort of head pain. Once I'd come back from a gig with a throbbing headache, probably from standing too close to the speakers, and she'd made me go see the doctor the next morning even though I was fine. It was so annoying.

'It's nothing!' I shouted when Mum came back, raging that she was sending me to the doctor again.

'Well, the doctor will be able to –'

'Mum, it's just a headache!' I went to storm out past her but the two of us got jammed in the tiny space. I tried to move by but we both went the same way and my bum bashed off hers.

'Stop laughing!' I screeched as I tried again to push her out of the way. But Mum couldn't stop, and soon her giggles turned into giant belly laughs and I was trying so hard not to laugh that my eyes were watering.

'Fine, I'll go to the bloody doctor!' I said when I'd eventually broken free, unable to contain my smile any longer.

Mum was busy organizing stuff for the house so I spent the

rest of the day alone, playing my guitar. I sounded pretty good as I'd been practising so much lately. At least there was one advantage to being totally bored.

It was warm in the caravan that night. I lay on top of my blanket in my white string top and pink pyjama shorts, staring at the ceiling. The road was eerily quiet. Not one car had passed in the last hour. The only sound was Mum's slow steady breathing. I reached for my phone to check the time. It was 2.15 a.m. and sure enough Emergency Use Only shone out from the corner of the screen.

I tried to sleep but was too warm to get comfortable. I sat up, slipped my feet into my pink Converse trainers, and tiptoed over to the door. Mum shuffled a bit in the bed but didn't wake. I shut the door softly behind me.

It was a lot cooler outside. I walked across the grass towards the house, sat down on the damp ground and stretched my legs out in front of me. I'd customized my trainers with little silver studs and they sparkled in the moonlight. It was a relief to breathe in the cooler night air. The caravan's ability to lock in the summer heat was really something. I ran my hands through the long tufts of grass and shut my eyes. I took in a deep breath of fresh air and gradually exhaled. And that's when I heard it. A sound that made me jerk upright.

I stood up and listened closely. It was coming from round the back of the house. Slowly I walked towards the noise, suspecting it was some sort of animal. I tiptoed so as not to scare it. The sound seemed to grow quieter as I got closer and the scraping became a soft scratch. I turned the corner into the back garden and scanned the darkness but I couldn't see anything. I listened more closely. It sounded like digging. It was coming from the far left-hand corner. I crept past the cement mixer and stepped over the pile of slates. Standing in the corner of the garden, I listened to the slow, steady digging sound. I no longer thought it was an animal. It was unmistakably the sound of a shovel digging into the ground. I looked around the garden, but there was nobody there. I checked behind the hedge but there was nothing there either. The sound definitely seemed to be coming from the back left corner, but there was nobody about. My heart started to beat loudly in my chest.

Horribly confused, I took one more look around, then decided to make my way back to the caravan. All of a sudden the stillness of the night seemed scary rather than peaceful. I managed to take a few steps but then a sick feeling suddenly struck the base of my stomach. The feeling crept up my throat, forcing the air out so that it was difficult to breathe. Terrified that I was about to faint, I sat down on the ground and put my trembling hands round my bare knees. I bowed my head and tried to take slow deep breaths, but sitting on the ground just made me feel worse. My body was weak and I couldn't see properly. I'd never felt like that before. I was so frightened that I tried to call out to Mum, but I could hardly breathe, let alone shout. I crawled into the centre of the garden. The further away I got from that back corner, the better I felt. Stones pierced the palms of my hands, but I barely noticed. A stale taste filled my mouth as I tried to gasp for air and tears streamed down my cheeks.

I could still hear the digging sound. It was getting louder now, filling my head so much that I couldn't even hear my own thoughts. I turned round but my vision was so blurred I couldn't make out anything in the darkness. Desperate to get back to the caravan I tried to get up but stumbled and fell back down to the ground. The digging was getting louder and louder and louder, a heavy shovel scraping against the earth, as though it were grating against the sides of my brain. I lay huddled on the ground, feeling as if I was waiting for my own grave to be dug, to be buried alive by this invisible suffocating presence. I covered my ears with my hands and tried to let out a scream, but it was so weak that nobody would be able to hear it. I pushed my palms against my ears and let out another desperate cry for help.

Then it stopped.

The sound just stopped, suddenly, as if someone had pushed the pause button on an iPod. My vision returned to normal and I frantically looked around the garden. There was nobody there. Even Mum hadn't heard my scream.

Eventually I felt strong enough to stand. I wiped my face and hurried back to the caravan. When I was safely inside I poured a glass of water and tried to wash the stale taste from my mouth.

'Are you OK, love?' asked Mum, sitting up in the bed and rubbing her tired eyes.

'Yes,' I lied. 'I was just in the bathroom.' She didn't notice that I was shaking. I held on to the edge of the counter for a moment, trying to understand what had just happened. Maybe something was wrong with me. The headaches, the nightmares . . . and now this. I couldn't explain it. I put my head in my hands and tried to make some sense of the incident. It was as if that desolate part of the garden had wiped all my energy. Maybe I'd imagined that noise. Lack of sleep had kicked my imagination into overdrive. I tried to convince myself that was it, but I knew I hadn't imagined it. I knew something very strange and very real had just happened.

I gulped down the water and took off my trainers, then got into bed and pulled up the covers. I had been too warm before, but now felt an icy chill. Maybe I was really sick after all. I tried to push the thought out of my head but it kept coming back. An hour later I finally drifted off to sleep, exhausted, and for once I was actually glad that Mum had made an appointment for me to visit a doctor.

Chapter 5

There was an emergency at the house, something to do with pipes, so Mum couldn't go with me to the clinic. I was secretly pleased about it as I could do without her fretting. I was still very creeped out by what had happened in the garden last night, but I tried not to think about it. I sat on the stone wall beside the bus stop, listening to Paramore on my iPod. The bus was late and my headache was still painful. My left eye throbbed as though it had a pulse of its own. I turned up the volume and tried to drown out the pain by concentrating on the words of the song. That helped whenever I was angry or nervous or frustrated. It was comforting to know that other people have similar problems, similar fears, similar desires. Sometimes it isn't comforting at all though. After I broke up with Cian I couldn't listen to any songs that mentioned love for at least a month. That rules out a lot of songs, trust me.

I heard my phone beep. It was a text from Ross.

Hey! I'm just in Temple Bar, waiting for Hannah. How are you? Miss ya.

I immediately felt jealous. We used to spend most Thursday mornings during summer sitting on the steps in Temple Bar

Square, waiting for Hannah to finish her acting class. We'd eat ice cream and listen to buskers and wander around Urban Outfitters looking at stuff we couldn't afford. I wished I was there now. But I had to stop torturing myself. I wasn't in Dublin, I was in Avarna, whether I liked it or not. I had to concentrate on making new friends.

I could see Sarah walking down the path towards me. I took out my earphones and smiled at her. 'Hey, Sarah, how are you?'

'Oh . . . hi,' she said, as if she didn't have a clue who I was. She gave me a really fake smile and kept walking.

Great, back to the torture chamber so. I put in my earphones and turned the music up even louder. It was probably for the best anyway. If she was actually nice to me, I'd feel even worse about fancying her boyfriend.

A few minutes later I felt someone tap my shoulder and looked up to see Colin. He looked very nice in dark denims and a red and blue striped T-shirt.

'What's up?' he said.

'I'm just waiting for the bus,' I replied, winding my earphones round my iPod and putting it in my bag. 'I have to go to the doctor in Drumshanbo.'

'Is something wrong?' He looked concerned.

'Just headaches. My mum is making me get them checked out,' I said, rolling my eyes.

'Oh, that sucks,' he said, kicking a pebble with the toe of his shoe. 'I'm so bored. Everyone's busy and there's nothing to do.'

'You could come with me, if you like? I can't promise it will be very exciting though.'

'Sure, why not,' said Colin. He began to count out his change. 'When's the bus due?'

'It should be here in a few minutes.'

He sat down next to me on the wall. 'Wanna play Would You Rather?'

'OK.'

Colin smiled. 'Right then, let me think. Would you rather . . . be able to read people's minds or know their future?' he asked, tilting his head.

'Read their minds,' I answered immediately. 'I don't think I'd like to know people's futures. Dealing with the present is hard enough without knowing what's coming next.'

'Interesting. Now you go.'

I thought hard, wanting to come up with something good. 'Would you rather . . . have to go to school naked for just one day, or have to go to school every day for the rest of your life?'

'Naked for one day. No question about it,' said Colin with a laugh. 'Would you rather find true love or find a million euro?'

I pondered it for a moment but the answer was obvious. 'True love,' I said. 'Would you rather . . . live without music or live without movies?'

'Music,' said Colin without hesitation. His answer surprised me. There was no way I could live without music. 'Would you . . . rather drown or be strangled to death?'

'Drown. Definitely.'

Forty minutes later we were sitting in the doctor's waiting room. It was a bit depressing, with a dark brown carpet, hard wooden chairs and a stack of magazines that were more than a year old. Colin sat beside me, flicking through one of them. An elderly woman in a navy headscarf sat across from me and a man with a toddler sat next to her.

'I can feel the germs in the air,' whispered Colin. 'That kid doesn't even cover his mouth when he coughs!'

'Colin, he's about two years old!'

'So?'

The little kid coughed again and Colin flinched.

Eventually a woman in a cream blouse and brown trousers called my name. Presumably Dr Cahill. I nodded and rose from my seat. She was petite, probably about sixty, with glasses and black curly hair. I followed her into the surgery, which was painted white with a black couch against the wall. Dr Cahill sat down on her leather chair, rested her hands on the desk and smiled at me. I had never been nervous in the doctor's before, but this time was different. This time there might actually be something seriously wrong with me. I tried not to think about that though. *Be positive*.

'I don't think we've met before, have we? I'm Dr Cahill.'

'No, we haven't,' I said, sitting down on the chair opposite. 'I'm Jacki King. My mum made the appointment. We've just moved here . . . Well, just moved to Avarna.'

'Oh, where in Avarna? I live near there,' she said, typing on her computer.

'Up by the mines. Alf Meehan's old house.' People still referred to it as Alf's. We'd probably have to be there a while before anybody called it the Kings' house.

'Ah yes. I heard that had been sold. Right, Jacki, what can I do for you?'

'Well, I've been having these headaches. My mum is worried because, as she told your receptionist, my dad died of a brain tumour.'

'I'm sorry to hear that, Jacki,' she said. 'I can understand why your mum might be worried, but it's probably nothing serious. Can you describe the headaches for me?'

I thought about how to explain them. 'Well, it's like an elastic band has been strapped round my head, and someone keeps pulling it tighter and tighter.' My headache had actually eased by now, but I'd never forget the pain.

'That's quite specific. OK, we'll check you for allergies. Something you're eating could be triggering them.'

Allergies. I liked the sound of that. It was a nice, logical explanation.

'Is there anything else?' asked Dr Cahill. I figured I might as well tell her about the other stuff. There was probably a simple explanation for that too.

'Well . . . I keep having this nightmare . . .' I began feeling slightly self-conscious. 'I have the same one every night . . .' I described the dream to her. When I'd finished she didn't say anything for a few moments. I was certain I saw a tinge of fear in her eyes. It made me very uneasy.

'Anything else?' she said.

'Well, I sort of had . . . like a panic attack or something . . . in the garden last night.' I told her about that too.

'The men from your dream . . . do you know them?' she asked, still staring at me intently.

'No. I've never seen either of them in my life.'

'Could you describe the men to me again?' she said.

I did. I described the man in the car with the frightening stare and the drunken man stumbling up the lane.

Dr Cahill typed something into her computer then turned back to me. 'Jacki, have you ever met Alf Meehan?' she asked.

'No.' It was a strange question. Immediately I thought of the threatening note I'd opened that was addressed to him and felt a chill. 'Why?'

'Because the drunk man you describe sounds exactly like him.' She stared at me again for a few moments then opened one of the drawers of the desk and took out a business card. 'There's someone else I'd like you to consult, Jacki. I think I know someone who might be able to help you.'

She handed me the card. It was cream with simple black and gold lettering. Printed on it was a mobile number, an Avarna address, and the words *Ger Rapple, Healer*.

A *healer*? It wasn't what I was expecting at all. 'What about the . . . the allergies?'

'I'd like to rule something else out first,' she said. 'I believe this may be outside my area.'

'What do you mean?' I was getting worried now. I didn't understand what was going on.

Dr Cahill lowered her voice. 'I think we may be dealing with something . . . something supernatural.'

I laughed. 'Um, OK.' I waited for the punch line, but she just continued to stare at me with an intense expression. 'What? Are you serious?'

'Trust me,' she said, standing up. 'Go and see Mr Rapple. I think he may be able to help.' She ushered me to the door. 'But do come and see me again if the symptoms persist.' She closed the door and I walked out of the clinic and into the street in a daze, forgetting Colin was with me.

'Jacki!' he called, rushing out after me. 'Are you OK? What did she say?' He looked concerned.

'She thinks it might be an allergy,' I said, avoiding eye contact with him. 'I have to get tests done.'

'Oh, right. Well at least you have an explanation now.'

'Yes . . . kind of.'

I don't know why I didn't tell Colin what the doctor had actually said. I guess I was still in shock. I'd gone to the doctor thinking she could help me, and all she'd done was give me the phone number of a healer. I didn't even believe in that sort of thing. The visit had been a complete waste of time.

'You're being very quiet,' Colin observed as we walked along.

'Am I?' I said, pushing Ger Rapple's business card further down in my jeans pocket.

I wanted to change the subject. I wanted to totally forget what had just happened.

'I saw Sarah earlier,' I said. I needed to talk about something normal.

'Oh, yeah . . . she's . . . she's nice,' said Colin, smiling half-heartedly. We arrived at the bus stop and I checked the times. There was one in six minutes.

'She kind of blanked me,' I said. 'Well . . . maybe she just didn't recognize me. I did only talk to her for a few minutes when I met her.'

'She's the most annoying girl who ever walked the planet,' said Colin in one breath, then covered his mouth with his hand. 'Oops,' he said, 'that just slipped out.'

'You don't like her?' I said, intrigued. I sat down on the path beside Colin.

He crossed his arms. 'I just find her really fake,' he said. 'I mean, yeah, she's gorgeous and all, but that doesn't give her the right to be so rude. She never makes an effort to talk to any of Nick's mates. She thinks she's better than all of us.'

'Maybe she didn't recognize me though, or maybe she thought I was being rude. I did kind of leave in a hurry the other day.' I didn't like to talk about people behind their backs, unless I was sure of my facts. It always came back to haunt me.

'I doubt you did anything wrong. I don't know any girls who like her. Worship her, yeah, terrified of her, yeah. But like her? No. Of course, most of the lads think she's all right. Pretty girls get away with so much. I'm sure you know that.'

I blushed. I didn't really see myself as pretty and got embarrassed when people referred to how I looked.

'Have they been going out long?' I asked, trying to sound as casual as possible.

'About four months, I think. That's the problem. He hasn't been going out with her long enough.'

'Long enough . . . for what?'

'Long enough to find out what she's really like: part stunner, part psycho.'

The way he said it made me laugh. 'He must really like her,' I said, thinking back to the way he'd looked at her in the shop.

'Oh yeah, he thinks he's totally in love with her.'

Great, that wasn't exactly what I wanted to hear. But it was sort of nice to know that Colin didn't like her.

'Crap, I need more change for the bus,' he said, digging around in his pockets.

I took out my purse to check what I had, but he'd already run off to a nearby shop.

He came out a minute later carrying two ice-cream cones.

'I hope you like sprinkles!' he said just as the bus pulled up.

Chapter 6

The next afternoon Colin had to help his mum in the guest-house, so I decided to write some lyrics. I needed to forget about what had happened at the doctor's the day before. That had really done my head in. I just couldn't accept that all that stuff was caused by something . . . What had she called it? Paranormal? Supernatural? Whatever it was, it was weird, but there was no way I was calling it any of those things. Maybe I was in denial, but I just couldn't go there. Mum had asked me how it went and seemed relieved when I used the allergies excuse again. I wasn't ready to tell her what Dr Cahill had really said.

I didn't need to think about that now; anyway I had more important things to consider. It was far too long since I'd written a song. The noise on the building-site-that-was-my-home wasn't making it the most inspirational place to write, so I threw my notebook into my patchwork bag along with my favourite pen, and headed for the village. I knew exactly where I'd go – to Avarna's communal garden. It was in a little hidden-away spot down by the river, the perfect place to write a song.

As I walked along the road I began to feel a bit better. I was happy with this plan. Arranging words to music has always been an important part of my life. After writing a song, I feel like a weight has been lifted from me, as if some of my deepest feelings have been released. I suppose you could say it's become my way of dealing with things. I find it much easier to write a song than to talk my problems over with somebody else. Putting the right words to my feelings seemed to make them more real, more permanent. Maybe that was why I found it so hard to find the words to describe what was happening . . . About what the doctor had said. I didn't believe in that kind of thing. I didn't want that to be part of my world, to consider the 'supernatural' a reality.

Love, on the other hand, was a totally different matter. I wanted that to be part of my life. I wanted it more than anything. I bent down and picked a daisy and pulled off the petals as I walked along. 'He loves me, he loves me not, he loves me, he loves me not, he loves me.'

I hurried down the path to the garden entrance, pushed open the white painted iron gate and stepped inside. The garden was surrounded by a low hedge. It was small but perfect, with a wrought-iron bench, a water fountain in the centre and a picnic table down near the river. I was glad to be alone in this miniature paradise.

A family of ducks floated on the river, the smallest one diving beneath the surface every few moments. The water was still except for the ripples made by the ducks. I was tempted to skim a stone and watch it bounce along the surface, but resisted. I didn't want to frighten them away.

A path led through the garden to the wrought-iron bench, which was under an oak tree. The iron felt cold against my back as I settled down, my patchwork bag beside me. Hundreds of people must have sat on this bench, each with their own stories, their own obsessions, their own pain. I took out my notebook and pen and started to write.

The words seemed to flow on to the page as easily as the river ran downstream. I like to just jot down whatever comes to me, not worrying whether it makes sense or not, and then work on it later. I read the words I'd just written, knowing that they were far from perfect, but knowing too that they reflected my feelings so, if nothing else, they were certainly honest.

When I thought about the last song I'd written it seemed like a lifetime ago. So much in my life had changed since then. I remembered it had been in Dublin, in my bedroom. I'd been so angry with Cian. I couldn't believe what he'd done. When I thought back now I wondered if maybe I'd been angry with myself for putting up with his crap for so long.

I looked up at the sky with its patches of blue and vast white and grey clouds, and for the first time I felt happy to be living here. Maybe I could adjust to country life after all. I loved the quietness, the sense of peace. I began to understand why so many people moved away from cities. Mary had told me that there were lots of creative types living in and around the village, artists and musicians who had been captivated by its tranquillity. Maybe my songs would get better now that I had such an inspiring place to write.

I picked another daisy and began plucking off its delicate white petals. Each one spiralled in the air before dropping on to my notebook.

'He loves me, he loves me not, he –'

The gate creaked. I looked up and was surprised to see Nick walking across the grass towards me, a guitar case slung across his back. Oh my god. I dropped the daisy to the ground and slammed the notebook shut. It was so weird to be thinking about someone so intensely, and then for them to show up out of nowhere.

'Hi, Jacki,' he said.

'Hey.' I was so surprised by his arrival that I didn't have time to get anxious about it. Nick looked like he hadn't got much sleep, but still managed to look irresistible.

'What's the story?' he said.

'Nothing much.'

'Are you going to the table quiz in the parish hall tonight?' He took his guitar off his shoulder.

'I don't know; maybe,' I said. I remembered Mum mentioning something about it the previous week. The idea of it hadn't exactly excited me.

'Well, if you do go, you can be on our team if you want. Sarah has to work so we're one short.'

I was suddenly most definitely going to the table quiz in the parish hall. I hoped that he hadn't noticed my face light up.

'OK . . . well, I'll most likely be there,' I said, as indifferently as possible.

'Right so. It starts at eight.'

I nodded. There was silence. Nick looked away, glancing awkwardly around the garden.

'Do you want to sit down?' I asked, moving my patchwork bag so that it didn't separate us.

'Sure.' He leaned his guitar against the end of the bench.

'Your mum was telling me you're pretty good at guitar,' I said, desperate to keep the conversation going.

'I'm all right, I guess. I play lead in my band. We were playing a gig in Sligo last night. I'm just back from there now.

54

Haven't slept in ages, as if you couldn't tell.' He smiled, then yawned and looked as if he might collapse from exhaustion any second.

'OK, so I won't take that personally then,' I joked. I wanted to add that I hadn't really slept either. But I didn't want to get into that. This was way too important. I was alone with Nick. I had to make the most of it, not start talking about supernatural nonsense. He didn't seem the type to believe in that kind of thing.

'What kind of guitar do you have?' I asked, steering the conversation towards something we had in common.

'An electric one, called a Fender Strat,' he answered, punctuating each syllable as if he were talking to a two-year-old.

'I have one of those too. I've been mainly playing acoustic lately though.'

Nick looked shocked. 'You play guitar?'

'A bit.'

'How long have you been playing?'

'Nearly five years now.'

'Are you in a band?'

'I've been in a few, but not at the moment.'

'Concentrating on your solo career?'

'I suppose I am,' I said with a laugh. This was going well.

'What's your favourite band?' he asked. He frowned and I knew a lot hinged on my answer.

'Ooh, that's a tough one . . .' I knew what he was doing – he was testing me. It was a way of separating the actual music lovers from the posers, i.e. the people who wore Ramones T-shirts but couldn't name any of their songs.

'I guess Thin Lizzy would be pretty high on the list,' I said.

'Class.'

'What about you? What's your favourite band?'

'Metallica,' he said, without hesitation.

'I'm not a hardcore fan,' I said. 'But they're unreal live.'

'You've seen them?'

'Yeah, I saw them in Marlay Park a few years ago.'

'Me too.' He smiled again. A perfect smile, I decided. He had nice teeth. And I noticed he hadn't shaved. I liked his rugged look. But I had to remind myself he was with Sarah. *Get a grip – he has a girlfriend.*

What followed was an intense conversation about iconic rock stars and guitar amps and distortion pedals. I had talked about them with countless guys in the past, so the words just fell out of my mouth. All I was thinking was how adorable Nick looked in that T-shirt, and how cute his smile was, and how much I desperately wanted to touch his lips with mine. Over the past few days I'd tried my best to stop fixating on this guy, who I barely knew, but now I realized that I couldn't fight it. It was official: he was just too perfect.

'What are you doing down here by yourself anyway?' he asked.

I had to force my thoughts back to the conversation.

'I was just writing some lyrics.'

'Really? Can I see them?'

'No. I mean . . . they're not finished yet . . . You can see them when they're finished.' I was reluctant to hand them over: they more than hinted at a sense of unrequited love. There was no way he was going to find out my true feelings, whether he recognized the inspiration or not.

'OK . . .' He yawned again and stood up. 'Well, I hope you can make it tonight.'

He hoped I could make it. When I like a guy, I tend to examine every word that comes out of his mouth with the determination of a profiler interviewing a suspect. He hoped I could make it. Perhaps things were not as bleak as they had originally seemed. He gave me another irresistible smile and headed back down the path towards the gate. He looked back once, and I really hoped he didn't catch me staring at him.

Once he'd left the garden I read the words of my new song again.

> *I know it would be perfect*
> *But you will never see;*
> *Your silent conversations*
> *Were never meant for me.*
> *When I think about it*
> *I shouldn't ache so bad.*
> *How can I miss something*
> *That I never had?*
>
> *Standing in this prison,*
> *I helped create my cell.*
> *How can a thing from heaven*
> *Make my life a hell?*
> *My heart's in little pieces;*
> *I must be going mad.*
> *How can I miss something*
> *That I never had?*

Yes. I'd definitely made the right decision not showing it to him.

It started to drizzle so I gathered my things and put them in my bag. I was glad the oak tree provided some shelter. I wanted this moment to last, so I closed my eyes. *He loves me, he loves me not, he really hoped I could make it, he loves me, he loves me not.* I stayed there for a few minutes, lost in my thoughts.

It was just a slight summer shower, so when it was easing off I got up and followed the path round to the water fountain on the other side of the oak tree. I watched the raindrops splash into it, joining the water that trickled down through the grey stone. The sound of the water had a wonderfully calming effect. I noticed there was a little brass plaque at the bottom of the fountain. Stepping closer I could see that the engraving on it read:

In memory of Beth Cullen, who spent happy times here.

There was that name again. If there was a fountain dedicated to her, she must have been very special. *Her family must really miss her*, I thought as I left the garden and headed back to the caravan.

Chapter 7

What does one wear to a Friday night table quiz in a parish hall? I wondered. I'd already spent almost two hours that evening trying to answer the question, and now I was running out of time. I wanted my style to be distinctive but understated. It was important to make an impression on Nick, but it should also look effortless. At the moment it looked like my suitcase had exploded, as I flung clothes all over the caravan.

'Jacki, will you come on? We're going to be late,' said Mum.

'OK, OK, I'm nearly ready.' Mum had got dressed in five minutes and looked perfect. She hardly spent any time on make-up whereas I couldn't go outdoors without eyeliner I felt so bare without it. My eyeliner had gone missing now and it took me about ten minutes to find it. And I still couldn't decide what to wear. Nothing looked right, nothing matched. Hannah and I usually got ready for important things together: we'd made a pact after the leggings incident of 09. They'd looked good in *Teen Vogue*, they'd looked good on the hanger, they had not looked good on me. After Hannah experienced a similar incident with denim hot pants, we'd made the pact. Mum was no help – she just said everything looked lovely. Maybe I could visit Dublin for a weekend soon . . . Hannah could come shopping with me. Clearly I desperately needed some new clothes.

I finally settled on my skinny jeans and white tank top with the gold detail and buttons down the front (top two left open). I quickly brushed my hair, lined my eyes black and slipped into my grey boots. I stuffed only the essentials – my purse, my phone and a stick of blood-red lipstick – into my black shoulder bag.

I stole one final glance in the bathroom mirror before following Mum out of the caravan on to the damp grass. It hadn't rained again but the sun was still hidden behind grey cloud. A light breeze carried us down to the village. Mum pulled her pink cardigan tighter round her shoulders as we dodged the puddles of rainwater dotted along the winding road. Avarna was beautiful in the daytime, but it was lovely in the evening too. It was so peaceful.

'You can be on our team if you want,' said Mum. 'A few other teachers from the school are going too.'

'It's OK. I already have a team.'

'Oh, really?'

'Nick from the shop asked me to join his. They were one short.'

'Nick from the shop, eh?' Mum stopped walking and gave me a quizzical look.

I couldn't stop my cheeks from going red.

'So that's why you took so long to get ready.'

'He has a girlfriend,' I said, walking ahead.

'Minor obstacle.'

'Mum!' I squealed, and we both laughed.

As we neared the parish hall the village was buzzing. Throngs

60

of people headed for the hall, located on the curve of the main street. It was hard to miss with its bright red window frames and doors. A large plaque with the numbers 1878 told us when it had been built and the COURTHOUSE sign informed us of its original function. I tried to imagine the trials that had gone on here in the past.

As we entered through the doors at the front of the building we could see groups gathered round the twenty or more tables across the floor. Whispers of gossip and bursts of laughter filled the hall. I could see Mary Reynolds weaving through the tables, placing a small stack of answer sheets on each as she passed. Quizmaster Joe Clancy was standing on the stage, surveying his audience. I spotted Nick at one of the tables at the front. Another guy sat across from him. I recognized Colin's red hair immediately. The minute I saw them I felt a bit nervous but I quickly got over it. This was too important to screw up.

'There's Margaret,' said Mum, waving over at the primary school principal. 'Is your team here yet?'

'Yep. They're over there,' I said, pointing at Nick.

'Oh, I see!' said Mum, raising an eyebrow at me. 'Good luck. And I hope you do well in the quiz too,' she added, smirking.

I rolled my eyes at her before strolling over to Nick and Colin. Nick was looking gorgeous, and had clearly got some sleep since I last saw him. He looked at me, and there was a noticeable second of silence – that momentary beat that every girl strives for, which can only be achieved through a perfectly planned outfit.

'Hi,' he said as his eyes subtly scanned my body. 'Colin, this is Jacki.'

'We've already met,' said Colin, looking up to smile at me.

There were ink stains on his hand and he was doodling with a biro.

'Oh, right. Take a seat.' Nick pointed to the grey chair next to him before glancing around the hall and then he began texting furiously. I dropped my bag to the floor and settled down. Nick's aftershave was almost overbearing, but so intoxicating that I wouldn't have minded being suffocated by it. He was wearing denims and a Metallica T-shirt. A red hoodie hung across the back of his chair.

'Four to a team, four to a team, twenty euro per table,' shouted Joe from the stage. 'Mary, will you see if you can get this to work?' he said as he fumbled with the faulty microphone. Mary hurried up the wooden steps on to the stage. Joe stood beside a long table in the middle of the stage, where a chubby man was seated.

'I didn't think this would be your kind of scene, Nick,' said Colin. 'I was expecting to have to drag you here.'

'Did you not know I was on our primary school quiz team?' he joked, acting insulted.

'Oh yeah, I forgot about that! But we'll hardly win without a full team . . .'

'I'll text Chris and see what's keeping him.'

'When is David back?' asked Colin, leaning back on his chair.

'Tomorrow. I've told you, like, eight times,' said Nick, without looking up from his phone. 'Don't worry, he got your comics or whatever it was you were looking for.'

'Aw, savage. Did he get all the ones on the list? And did he get that DVD I asked for?'

'I don't know. I was only talking to him online for a few minutes.'

'He's so lucky. I'd literally kill to go to Japan.' Colin picked up his phone and started texting.

'Who's David?' I asked, wanting to get in on the conversation.

'Our mate,' said Colin. 'His dad has businesses all over the place and is always going away. He had to go to some conference in Japan and David got to go with him. His dad is a bit of an asshole; David's sound though. And his sister Carla is all right sometimes.'

'He's not an asshole,' said Nick, dropping his phone down on the table. 'Peter Mulvey is one of my dad's best friends.'

'Whatever,' said Colin, turning to me and rolling his eyes.

'Twenty euro, please,' said the woman who had just arrived at our table.

Nick's phone buzzed. He read the message and sighed. 'Chris can't come – he's stuck in work. Looks like it's just the three of us, so that's going to be . . .' Nick attempted the mathematics in his head.

'Six sixty-seven each!' I said. I loved maths. Maths and music were my two favourite subjects.

'Eh . . . yeah,' he muttered. We handed the woman our money.

'David lives up near Nick,' said Colin. 'You'll get to meet him when he gets back.'

'Testing, testing,' Joe's voice echoed through the hall's speakers. 'Good evening, ladies and gentlemen. Welcome to the G. A. A. club's annual table quiz. As usual there will be ten rounds and prizes will be given for the teams who come first, second and third. Alec McNamara, your local accountant –' Joe pointed to the man seated next to him – 'will be keeping the scores tonight.' Alec gave a nod to the crowd. A black calculator and a row of sharply pointed pencils were positioned neatly on the desk in front of him.

'Please write your table number clearly on the top of each answer sheet, and hand them to the lovely Mary Reynolds at the end of each round.' Mary gave a little wave to the crowd. 'The best of luck to everyone,' said Joe. 'We'll be starting shortly.'

Nick shuffled about in his seat, and for a split second his leg touched mine. It's amazing how electrifying a touch can be when it comes from someone you really like.

Nick saw that Colin was holding a pen and had resumed his doodling, so he placed the bundle of paper in front of him.

'You can write the answers,' he said. 'We're table four.'

I watched as Colin began to print the number four clearly at the top of each sheet.

'Right, round one,' Joe's voice hushed the crowd. We huddled together like a guerrilla group preparing to go into battle, each of us displaying that fiercely competitive streak that surfaces in even the most placid of people during the marvel that is the table quiz.

'Question one.'

We leaned in closer together.

'Who is the Roman goddess of love?'

During these huddles my head was dangerously close to Nick's. I noticed how long his eyelashes were.

'A haematologist specializes in the study of what?'

And how a freckle touched the centre of his top lip.

'If you have myopia, what would you suffer from?'

And how there was hard skin on his fingertips from playing guitar.

'Jacki . . . Jacki!' Colin whispered loudly as he tugged at my arm.

'Oh, sorry.' I'd been entirely absorbed in my own thoughts and hadn't heard the question.

'Do you know what it is? Which spirit is used in a bloody Mary?'

I realized that I would have to stop thinking about how close I was to Nick and focus on Joe's questions. After all, I did want to get at least a few questions right, or Nick would think I had no general knowledge.

'It's vodka,' I whispered to Colin.

At the interval tea and biscuits were served. We seemed to have done moderately well in the first half, though not as well as I'd hoped. The questions were far more difficult than I'd antici-pated. And of course I was distracted. No matter how hard I tried, I couldn't seem to keep my eyes off Nick for more than a few seconds.

'I'm going to get tea. Does anyone want anything?' I asked.

Nick shook his head.

'I'll have a cup of coffee,' said Colin. 'A caramel frappuccino if they have it,' he added with a smile.

'I'll see what I can do,' I said with a laugh.

The refreshment table was at the back of the hall, so I started to battle my way through the crowd.

'Is Lily coming tonight?' an old lady in front of me asked her grey-haired companion as they approached the table. They were walking slowly and the two kids behind me were pushing so much I came uncomfortably close to the old ladies' perms. The smell of hairspray filled my nostrils.

'No, she didn't feel up to it. She misses Jim terrible, God rest him.'

'He died very sudden, didn't he, Molly?'

'Oh yes, very sudden. It was quite a shock to us all . . . Can't be easy for her, what with Beth's birthday coming up and everything. Two teas, please, Angela.'

Beth. There was that name again.

'What would you like, love?' said the lady behind the table as I approached.

'A tea and a coffee, please,' I said.

She poured them into two paper cups.

'How much is that?'

'Nothing. It's free,' she said.

Pleasantly surprised, I thought I ought to take a few biscuits too.

I fought my way back through the crowd and arrived with the cups and a fistful of biscuits. Nick was gone, presumably to the bathroom. As I approached our table, Colin, not noticing me coming, pushed his seat back to stand up. It was one of those situations that I could see happening in slow motion, but I was powerless to stop it. I managed to save the tea but the coffee splashed on to my top, turning the white to a muddy brown.

'Argh!' I blurted as the warm liquid seeped down my front.

'I'm so sorry!' said Colin, jumping up. 'Are you OK? Are you burnt?'

'No, it's fine. Thankfully it's not too hot.' I put the tea down on the table. 'I think I'll have to go home and change though. It's soaking.'

'But the second half is about to start,' said Colin, clearly upset. 'Here, you can wear my shirt. No one will even notice.'

Colin pulled off the check shirt he was wearing over the white T-shirt and gave it to me.

'Oh . . . OK, thanks.' Colin was being so nice . . . I didn't want him to feel bad about what happened so I took him up on the shirt offer.

I followed the signs for the toilets and arrived at the single cubicle. I joined the queue of five ladies waiting by the lime-green door. In front of me stood a woman and a young girl, probably aged four, with her light blonde hair sectioned into two neat plaits. She was singing quietly to herself while her mother chatted to the woman in front.

'Miss Jane had a bag
And a mouse was in it.
She opened the bag;
He was out in a minute.
The cat saw him jump
And run under the table
And the dog said –'

'And, Lisa, how are you?'

The little girl looked up at the woman who was talking to her mother, and now to her.

'Fine,' she said sheepishly, and retreated behind her mother's leg.

'Ah, someone's shy!' said the woman. The girl resumed singing softly.

'Miss Jane had a bag
And a mouse was in it . . .'

I was back in time for the second half, wearing the oversized shirt, and clutching my soaking wet top. So much for the perfectly planned outfit. I sat back down beside Nick.

'I heard Colin didn't like his frappuccino?' he whispered.

I laughed but there was no time to respond as Joe tapped the microphone and the hall fell silent.

'Round six, everyone, pencils ready.'

We huddled closer.

'What famous song did the Hill Sisters write?'

The three of us looked baffled. Nick squinted his left eye when he was thinking.

'Arsonphobia is a fear of what?'

And bit the nail on his right thumb.

'A currier works with which material?'

And he smiled a little whenever he knew the answer.

The atmosphere in the hall was gradually tensing as the teams tried to make up for their mistakes in the first half. We picked up between us in the showbiz round and Nick knew all the answers in the sports round.

'The final round is a bonus round, double points will be awarded for each question,' said Joe. 'Question one: in what year did work cease in the Avarna mines?'

Nick struggled to remember, his head now resting in his hand.

'How many sheep are currently grazing in Maurice Kelly's field?'

Colin rolled his eyes.

'How many times has Avarna won the Tidiest Village title?'

Nick sighed.

'What is the colour of the doormat in Mary Reynolds's shop?'

'Green,' said Nick and I in unison.

'Think we're in with a chance?' said Nick when Mary had collected the last of the answer sheets.

'Doubt it,' said Colin. 'That Avarna round let us down. No one ever beats Father McCauley and the Eucharistic Ministers anyway.' He pointed to a table on the other side of the hall where Avarna's parish priest was looking particularly confident.

'Sorry again. About the coffee,' said Colin.

'It's OK, don't worry about it.' Secretly I hoped I'd be able to get the stain out. It was one of my favourite tops. I rolled up the shirt's sleeves, trying to make it look a bit girlier.

'Back in a minute, scuse me,' Colin said as he left the table.

'Sorry if this wasn't very exciting,' said Nick.

'What? Are you kidding? I had a great time!' It had been a lot of fun. I didn't want it to end.

'Well, if you thought this was good, wait till you experience the Avarna Fête next Sunday.'

'Oh, really?'

Nick nodded. 'They have it every year,' he said. 'I've had to listen to Mam going on about it all month. She helps organize it.'

'Does she help organize everything?' I joked.

'Pretty much. She likes to keep busy. Anyway . . . you should come to the fête. David and a few of the lads will be there. I'll introduce you.' He smiled. That irresistible smile got me every time.

'I will . . . probably. I was going to visit my friends in Dublin next weekend . . . but I might just stay here.' I did want to see Hannah and the others, but I also really wanted to make new friends. And I really wanted to hang out with Nick.

'Did I miss anything?' asked Colin, coming back to the table.

'No, they haven't announced the results yet,' said Nick.

'Testing! Testing!' said Joe.

'Here we go,' said Colin. 'Fingers crossed.'

We finished an admirable third, beaten by Mum and her team of teachers in second place and Father McCauley's team in first. Nick, Colin and I were each given a box of biscuits from Mary's shop as a prize. Nick was noticeably unimpressed. Mum's team won the hamper and the priest's team got vouchers for Sunday dinner in the hotel.

'That's it, folks! Everyone is welcome to join us in Clancy's!' said Joe.

I looked around to try to spot Mum. She was probably going to the pub with her teammates.

I reluctantly got up from my seat. I really didn't want to leave Nick. I liked being near to him even if I knew that I couldn't do anything . . . But it was nice being that close. Close enough to touch. *Even though you can't*, I said to myself.

'That was great craic,' said Colin. 'Sure isn't a nice box of biscuits better than nothing, Nick!'

Nick pushed him and Colin ran ahead.

'Jacki, are you coming to the pub?' asked Nick.

I was now.

Chapter 8

'Looks like they've got a bit of a sing-song going,' said Colin. Mary, Joe and some others had formed a circle round the tables in the centre of Clancy's and had just launched into a rendition of 'Danny Boy'.

'I love this song!' said Mary, singing at the top of her lungs. Soon nearly everyone in the pub had joined in. I hummed along during the breaks in our conversation. Tonight had been so much fun up until now, but it had just taken a turn for the worse. Sarah had arrived, and she and Nick were whispering away to each other beside us. She was wearing a denim mini-skirt and a pale pink tank top and looked annoyingly pretty. I kept glancing at them, even though watching Sarah groping Nick was torture. I hated being jealous. It was one of the worst feelings in the world. My stomach was all twisted and I couldn't think straight. I didn't want to feel like this, but I couldn't help it. I tried to hear what they were saying.

'Will I show you my dress tomorrow?' said Sarah.

'Yeah, OK.'

'You don't seem that interested.'

'No, I am. I am,' said Nick, taking a sip from his drink and looking around the crowded pub. Colin lowered my glass of Coke under the table and poured some vodka from his naggin into it. Joe had made an exception and allowed us to sit in the pub because of the night that it was, but there was no way he was going to allow us to order alcohol.

'There's a lot of competition this year,' said Sarah.

'I'm sure you'll win,' said Nick, disinterest evident in his voice.

'Win what?' asked Colin.

'The Miss Avarna pageant,' said Sarah, clearly expecting us to say something.

'You know, the beauty contest they have at the fête,' said Nick.

'It's so much more than a beauty contest!' Sarah protested, shooting him an irritated glare. 'They ask questions and –'

'Is it time for the fête already?' Colin interjected, trying to keep a straight face. Sarah still seemed to be waiting for someone to say how she was going to win.

I took a sip from my vodka and Coke, avoiding eye contact with Colin, who would have made me laugh.

'Yes, it's on next Sunday,' said Nick.

'Oh, right,' said Colin. 'Jacki, you should enter.'

I almost choked on my drink.

'Closing date for entries was last week,' said Sarah abruptly, flicking her black hair over her shoulder.

'I don't think it would really be my kind of thing anyway,' I said. 'I'd probably end up saying something really weird and embarrassing myself.' I didn't like the idea of people judging my personality – I did enough judging of it myself.

'What will we sing next, Joe?' shouted Mary. She was really

into the sing-song. I bet Mum would have enjoyed it too, but in the end she'd gone home because she had to get up early to meet the kitchen suppliers.

I texted to let her know we were enjoying a sing-song and that I'd be home in a while.

Joe thought for a moment, then launched into –

'I'll tell me Ma when I go home the boys won't leave the girls alone . . .'

Colin leaned over to me. 'You'd beat Sarah anyway,' he whispered. I doubted that very much, but I appreciated Colin's remark nonetheless.

'What do you get? If you win?' I asked Sarah.

'A trophy. And a spread in the paper. And the honour of being Miss Avarna, of course.'

Colin was trying so hard not to laugh. He elbowed my side and I kicked his shoe in retaliation, hoping Sarah wouldn't notice.

'What do you have to do?' I asked, stifling a giggle.

'Well,' she said, 'there are three judges, and they ask you a few questions about yourself, and then a few random ones, about politics and human rights and all that stuff. Then there's a talent section.'

'Like in the Rose of Tralee? When they do a dance or read a poem or something?'

'Yes. Exactly.'

'What are you going to do?' asked Colin.

'Sing a song.'

'Oh, very good. Which one?'

'"When Irish Eyes Are Smiling". They like when you pick a traditional one. My cousin Ailish was apparently winning last

73

year until she did some sort of rap and it totally went over the judges' heads. My sister won it before. She's been giving me pointers.'

'Can we talk about something other than the beauty contest?' said Nick.

'Nick, it's so much more than a beauty contest,' said Colin dramatically, although Sarah was completely oblivious to his sarcasm. Sometimes I considered the advantages of being that self-absorbed.

The crowd got louder as everyone joined in the chorus.

> *'She is handsome, she is pretty,*
> *She is the belle of Belfast city.*
> *She is a-courtin' one, two, three,*
> *Please won't you tell me, who is she?'*

The atmosphere in the pub was brilliant. The drinking and the singing and the chatting continued beyond closing time. I didn't want to leave. I was having the most fun I'd had in ages. Just being around Nick gave me a little shiver of excitement. I should have felt bad thinking this way when his girlfriend was sitting less than a metre away, but she was being so irritating that I found my guilt fading.

'I'm going to get some crisps,' I said. I'd been so excited at the prospect of being on Nick's table quiz team that I hadn't been able to eat much earlier.

'Oh, will you get me some too?' Colin asked.

'Sure,' I said, and made my way over to the bar.

'Some of those questions were impossible, Joe,' said Mary. Joe was standing behind the bar with his wife, Rita.

'What year did Phil Lynott die?' said Rita, flicking through Joe's quiz sheets. 'I should know that.'

'1986,' I said involuntarily. Thin Lizzy trivia was one of my specialities.

'That was the year I got married,' said Mary. 'And the year Beth Cullen was murdered.'

Murdered? This was too weird. Not only did I keep coming across her name, but she'd been murdered. The combination of the two was unsettling.

'Is it that long ago?' said Rita, collecting empty glasses from the counter.

'Yes,' said Joe. 'Twenty-five years. Hard to believe, isn't it? God rest her soul.' He blessed himself and turned to me. 'What can I get for you, Jacki?'

'Er . . . J-just two packets of crisps, please, Joe,' I stammered, and handed over some change. I made my way back to our table and I noticed there was a stool next to Colin.

'Who was Beth Cullen?' I asked him as we opened our crisps.

'Jim and Lily Cullen's daughter. She was best friends with Lydia too, actually. She was murdered in 1986 around Christmastime and her body was found a week later in the forest.'

'Oh my God . . .' I said as a chill crept up my back. 'How old was she?'

'She was twenty-two. They had a huge search party out looking for her from the very night she went missing. Her parents found her bike dumped up by the church, and they knew straight away that something was wrong.'

'But it took a week to find her?'

'That forest is more than four hundred hectares. They found her not far from your house actually.'

75

I shivered at the thought of a dead body being discovered near my house, even if it had been twenty-five years ago. 'Thanks, Colin,' I said. 'Did you really need to tell me that? I'm having nightmares as it is!'

'Don't worry. All this happened before either of us was born, remember. But I've heard lots about it because my mam and dad were part of the search party. Lydia couldn't face it though. She was in shock because Beth was her best friend and she was afraid of finding her. She said she knew she was already dead. From the day she went missing she knew something terrible had happened.'

'How?'

'I don't know . . . just an instinct, I guess.'

I didn't feel like eating my crisps. I just didn't feel hungry any more. Suddenly, in my head was a vision of Beth Cullen's body, preserved by the cold December air, hair tangled across her face, hiding her features, her skin as pale as porcelain, her eyes still open, staring straight ahead, frozen in fear.

I couldn't believe I'd just conjured up an image like that in my head. It wasn't like anything I'd seen on TV or in movies. I didn't even know what she looked like, but it was horribly detailed. Horribly real. I had an unsettling sick feeling in my stomach.

'Who murdered her?' I asked, pushing my crisps aside.

'No one knows,' said Colin. 'They never caught the psycho.'

'But they must have had some suspects or at least –'

'Here, one of these young ones will give us a song!' shouted Mary, pointing over at our table.

'No, you're all right, Mam,' said Nick.

'Ah, go on! Don't be shy,' said Joe.

'Sarah, go on and give us a song there,' said Colin. 'It'll be good practice for your pageant.'

'OK then,' she said, sitting up straight and fixing her hair. She started to sing softly.

'*When Irish eyes are smiling . . .*'

'God help Nick if she doesn't win this Miss Avarna thing,' whispered Colin. 'She'll be crying for a fortnight.'

I didn't like to admit it but Sarah's voice was very sweet and she seemed to be extremely well prepared – and she was pretty.

There was a round of applause. Sarah smiled.

'Well done!' said Nick.

'Jacki,' said Lydia. 'Your mam told me you're a great singer. Will you sing something for us?'

'Yeah, go on, Jacki!' said Mary.

'Oh, all right . . . OK,' I said. I loved singing. I glanced over at Nick. He was still congratulating Sarah.

'What are you going to sing?' said Colin.

I thought about it for a moment, then the perfect song came into my head.

'I think I'll do "She Moved Through the Fair".'

'Oh, I really like that song,' said Colin.

People were often surprised when they heard me sing. I guess my voice was quite different to how I looked. I closed my eyes and began.

> '*My young love said to me, my mother won't mind*
> *And my father won't slight you for your lack of kind . . .*'

I could feel Nick looking at me as I sang. Thankfully I was used to performing and it didn't make me too nervous.

When I finished there was a moment of silence and then lots of loud applause.

'Whoa, you've got some voice there,' said Joe.

'Thanks,' I replied, a little embarrassed because everyone in the pub was staring at me.

'That was brilliant,' said Colin.

'It really was,' agreed Nick.

'Thanks.'

'Your voice is so distinctive,' said Lydia. 'So effortless.'

I tried not to blush.

'I've heard that song so many times before,' said Colin. 'But I never really listened to the words until now. You're a great singer.'

Then looking at Sarah, he added, 'Oh . . . you were great too, Sarah.'

She looked at him blankly.

'Seriously though,' said Colin, turning to me. 'I'm your new number one fan. Can I design your album cover when you're famous?'

'Ha, sure,' I promised.

'Simon just texted me,' said Nick. 'Himself and the lads are having a few cans up in the forest. Will we head up to them?'

'All right,' said Colin. 'You'll come too, won't you, Jacki?'

'Where?' I asked.

'The forest. There's a clearing up behind the mines, just past your house. We hang out there sometimes.'

'Yeah, sure, I'll come.' I couldn't help thinking back to Beth Cullen. Not that it mattered – I was hardly going to be wandering around there in the dark on my own. Anyway, there was nothing to be afraid of.

Nick's phone buzzed again. He stared at the screen for a few moments, a look of confusion on his face. Then he turned to Sarah.

'Babe, what's this?' he asked, showing her the phone.

She took a few seconds to answer, and suddenly looked very flustered.

'Em . . . I . . . I can explain; it's not what –' She put her hand on his arm.

'Is it a joke?' he said, looking at the screen again.

'Listen, Nick, I was wasted . . . I didn't –'

'So you're not even denying it?' he said, pushing her hand away. 'I don't believe this.' Then he stuffed his phone in his pocket and hurried towards the door.

'Nick, wait!' shouted Sarah, running after him.

'What was that all about?' I said.

'Dunno,' said Colin. 'They're always fighting. Come on, let's go to the forest. They'll catch up.'

Chapter 9

We turned left before the disused Avarna coal mines and followed a path that led to the forest. It was so dark I could hardly see beyond the narrow conifers in front of me. Once we ventured into the forest, the path wound and turned and I couldn't tell in which direction we were heading. I struggled to keep up with Colin, who knew this section of the forest so well that he could find his way easily in the darkness. I followed a metre or so behind, using my phone as a torch, careful not to trip over any protruding roots. Twigs snapped under my feet and the occasional sound rustled in the treetops above my head.

There was still no sign of Nick or Sarah. If that fight was anything like the ones Cian and I used to have, it would probably go on for ages. I still couldn't believe how much time I'd wasted arguing with him. Deep down I must have known I was unhappy, but I just couldn't let him go. And when I finally broke up with him I wasted even more time. I locked myself in my room and did nothing except eat giant chocolate buttons, listen to non-love songs and read music biographies. Mum had tried to coax me out with the promise of shopping trips, but eventually she'd given up.

Hannah had wanted to throw me a break-up party (she'd

never liked Cian), but I refused to leave my room. That's a week of my life I'll never get back. Although I did get through quite a few biographies. I now know that Patti Smith was superstitious and that Kurt Cobain liked to collect heart-shaped boxes. If I ever get famous, I pity the person who has to write my biography. When they look through my life they won't find many interesting facts or quirky details. But I suppose I do have the standard dysfunctional relationship to my name.

I've always been amazed at how strange a thing love can be. It can steal all sense of logic from even the smartest of people. I was pretty sure Sarah was not 'the one' for Nick, but I knew how relationships worked, so I wasn't expecting him to realize that any time soon. At least Colin agreed that she wasn't right for him. But who was I to know what was really going on? I barely knew either of them.

'Hey, wait up,' I said as I hurried through the darkness. Colin was resting against one of the tree trunks, waiting until I caught up.

'What's that over there?' I asked, pointing to our left where four small wooden crosses stood at the head of a large flat grey stone.

'Famine grave,' said Colin as we walked on.

Shivering at the thought of treading over another person's bones, I stepped on the ground as softly as possible. I'd already decided that I was going to be cremated rather than buried. I didn't like the thought of being stuck underground. The notion of my ashes floating around some place special was much preferable. Not that I'd know the difference when I was dead. But, still, I knew I didn't want a grave.

'Are we near where Beth's body was found?' I asked.

'No, that was much further in. Don't worry, we're just head-ing for the clearing. We're almost there.'

'I'm not worried,' I said, but the image of Beth Cullen's murdered body haunted me. I just couldn't stop thinking about how I'd imagined her – her tangled hair, her eyes frozen in a deathly stare.

'They're just over here,' said Colin, rushing ahead again. It was taking all my concentration not to trip over, so I didn't even bother to catch up with him.

I could hear laughter up ahead, then a guy's voice.

'Colin, you know that girl you were on about? The one whose mother bought Alf's house?' They were talking about me. I hadn't been nervous about meeting everyone before, but I was actually worried now. I wondered what this guy was going to say about me. Had he taken an instant dislike to me without even meeting me?

'Yes. Actually she's –'

'I got a good look at her today. Nick was right. She's hot.' My heart thumped faster. Had I heard that right? I slowed down a bit, wondering what else this guy would say.

'Shh,' whispered Colin. 'She's right h–'

'I heard she was in your house the other day. Maybe you could introduce me?'

I couldn't believe what I'd just heard. I stepped into the clear-ing where four people sat round a small campfire. The guy looked shocked.

'Sure,' said Colin. 'Simon, meet Jacki. Jacki . . . meet Simon.'

Simon turned bright red with embarrassment.

I nodded at him but he quickly turned away. So Nick Reynolds thought I was hot. I couldn't believe it.

'Aren't you going to introduce us too?' said the dark-haired guy sitting on Simon's right.

'Jacki, this is Chris,' said Colin.

Chris had several tattoos on his left arm and a lip piercing.

'Hi,' he said, and then took a sip from his can of cider. I nodded at him.

'And this is Fitz.'

'Hey,' I said.

Fitz took a pull on his spliff and nodded at me. He had scruffy blond hair and bright blue eyes.

'And this is Emily.'

'Hi!' said Emily with a smile. She was a pretty girl with dyed red hair and was wearing a black hoodie, purple skinny jeans and a little black bow in her hair. I instantly liked her.

'How was the table quiz?' asked Emily as we joined the circle.

'It was fun,' I said. 'We came third.' I sat down between Emily and Colin. The campfire crackled in front of us.

'A table quiz?' said Fitz. 'Ye're such nerds.'

'Shhh!' said Emily, obviously worried that he might offend me.

'Chill out, Em,' said Fitz. 'Not everyone is as sensitive as you.'

Emily gave Fitz the finger without looking at him, and then asked me lots more questions. I really liked her. She was one of those people who made you feel comfortable, even though you didn't know them at all.

'Suppose you won't want any of the nerdy biscuits we won then, Fitz,' said Colin, opening his tin. Fitz swiped a chocolate one and Colin wrestled him to the ground. Fitz almost kicked Emily by mistake, but she dodged his foot just in time.

'They can be SO annoying,' she said, but she didn't actually seem mad. Chris threw a stick on to the campfire. His tattoos were really cool. It was very unfair that Mum wouldn't let me get even a tiny one.

'Did you guys hear about Nick and Sarah?' said Chris.

'Yeah, what's up with them?' said Colin, abandoning the struggle, and brushing dirt off his denims. 'They had a bit of a row in the pub. Nick seemed pretty mad.'

'Well, he should be,' said Emily. 'She cheated on him.'

'No way!' said Colin.

It took a few seconds for what she had just said to register in my brain . . . No. Way.

Emily took out her phone and showed us a picture of what appeared to be Sarah attached to the face of some spiky-haired guy. 'She ran into him at her cousin's eighteenth in Dublin last week. Someone's sister took this photo of them and sent it to Emma, who sent it to Carla's cousin, who sent it to Carla, who sent it to me.'

'So they're finished then?' I asked, maybe a little too eagerly. I felt bad for Nick, because I knew what it felt like to be cheated on. But I also felt unbelievably happy.

'I reckon so,' said Chris. This was shaping up to be the best night in a long time.

Chris handed me a can of cider and cracked one open for himself. I pulled Colin's shirt tighter around me. I was cold but I didn't care. Nick and Sarah were finished. And there was even a possibility that he might like me. I couldn't believe my luck. And this was my first time out past midnight since we'd moved to Avarna. It was great just to be somewhere other than the caravan. Mum had a habit of going to bed annoyingly early, so the past few weeks I'd only had my iPod for company after eleven. I loved just sitting here talking. We chatted about random things, our conversation spattered with shouts of disagreement and blasts of laughter.

'Damn, you look good,' Colin told his reflection in my owl-shaped pocket mirror.

'Give me that!' I said. My eyeliner had completely rubbed away and the spot on my forehead that I'd so carefully concealed earlier was starting to show again. I wanted to look my best, just in case Nick arrived.

'Don't worry, Jacki, you look great,' said Colin, flipping the mirror closed and throwing it into my lap. 'Sure you've already impressed Simon over there. What more could you want?'

Simon still couldn't look me in the eye, and he went really red when I tried to make conversation with him. I gulped down the remainder of the can. I was starting to feel kind of nauseous after the vodka and Coke in Clancy's. What was I thinking, mixing my drinks? That never ended well.

Chris lit a cigarette and offered me one.

'No, thanks,' I said.

'Jacki doesn't smoke – she's a singer,' explained Colin.

'Wow, cool!' said Emily. 'I wish I could sing. I've never sung in front of anyone.'

'I can sing,' claimed Fitz. It was the first thing he'd said in about twenty minutes.

'Ha, no, you can't,' said Simon with a snort.

Fitz took a deep breath, and then sang a few bars of 'Bohemian Rhapsody' impressively well.

'Fitz, you legend,' said Colin. 'Apologize to the man, Simon.'

'I stand corrected,' admitted Simon.

'*I* know,' said Chris, 'Let's play I Never!'

'What's that?' asked Emily, running her fingers through the pine needles beside me.

'Well, basically you say something you've never done, like "Never have I ever . . . been caught by my parents getting stoned." Then whoever has actually done the thing you said, has to drink. Like, if you had said that, Fitz would have drunk.'

'Never have I ever . . . stolen something,' said Chris. I'd never stolen anything ever. Nothing. Not even a jellybean when everyone else was stealing them from the sweet stand in the cinema. There was no way I could do it. Weird? Maybe.

Chris drank, Simon drank, Emily didn't drink, Colin didn't.

'Never have I ever . . . got so drunk that I passed out,' said Simon.

I didn't drink. I'd never let myself go that far.

Colin drank, Chris drank, Emily didn't.

'Never have I ever had sex in the back of a car,' said Fitz.

I didn't drink for that one either. Not only had I never had sex in a car, I'd never had sex anywhere. Hopefully nobody would say that one.

Simon was the only one who took a mouthful from his can. I had a feeling he was bluffing.

'Never have I ever kissed more than one person on the same night,' offered Emily.

I drank. It was at a school disco when I was thirteen. I kissed my boyfriend at the time, then some random guy when my boyfriend went off with another girl. Those discos were never as good as we hyped them up to be.

86

Then it was my turn to think up something. 'Never have I ever . . . had a crush on one of my teachers.'

Nobody drank, except for Emily.

'*What?*' she said. 'Am I the only one? We have a really hot English teacher!'

One can of cider later and I was way past my limit. Usually I didn't drink much at all. I was talking too loudly, and stuff that wasn't even remotely funny seemed absolutely hilarious.

Chris twisted the tab of his beer can until it came off, then he flicked it away. I watched as it landed beside my shoe. My mind was sort of spinning so I rested my head on Colin's shoulder. At least I'd forgotten about my headaches and nightmares and about what the doctor had said. I hadn't forgotten about Nick though. There was still no sign of him, but I couldn't give up hope that he would turn up. I would have given anything to see him walking out from those trees.

Simon came over and sat between Emily and me. I guess he'd got over his earlier embarrassment. I was beginning to regret that I'd drunk so much as he was being really chatty, but all I could think about was how unwell I was feeling. Had I really had that much to drink?

'Are you all right?' he said, shifting away slightly.

'Yes . . . I'm fine . . . Think I'll just go for a little walk in the woods.' I tried to sound casual. 'I'll be back in a minute,' I said, making my way over to the trees.

Colin called after me but I kept going.

My vision was getting blurry, just like it had in the back garden, and there was a stale taste in my mouth. Then something moved over to my right. The trees rustled and I heard someone walking behind me.

'I'm OK,' I said. 'I'll be back in a minute.'

But the footsteps kept going, past me and then further into the trees.

'Who's that?'

There was still no reply. I followed the footsteps. I'm not sure why, but something told me to. I could see a grey figure moving quickly through the trees up ahead. It would vanish for a second and then re-emerge, weaving in and out between the tree trunks. It moved very fast. Unnaturally fast. I quickened my pace, jogging in the same direction. After a few moments it slowed down and stood still. I was getting closer to it. Part of me said turn back, but another part said to keep on running. As I got closer I could make out the frame of a woman – slim and tall with long black hair, but I couldn't distinguish her features. She was close but I just couldn't focus on her face. I stopped maybe a metre away, squinting through the darkness.

'Who's that? I asked. 'Who's there? Who are you?'

She didn't stay still for long. She came towards me and sped past. I jumped back and stumbled on a root, landing hard on the ground.

'Are you OK?' said Colin. I looked up to see him and Simon standing behind me.

'Yes, I was just . . . the girl.' I looked around, but couldn't see her. I couldn't understand how somebody could move that quickly.

'We were worried there for a second. We thought we heard a scream.' I didn't remember a scream. Maybe I'd cried out when I'd hit the ground. My arm was grazed, but I was so confused I didn't feel the pain.

'Where's she gone?' I said. I looked around again, but she wasn't there any more.

'Who?' said Colin.

'There was a girl here. I . . . I saw a girl.'

Simon leaned over and looked into my eyes. 'What did you take?' he said. Great, I was acting so weird he thought I was on something. But I knew I'd definitely seen her.

'She didn't take anything!' said Colin, pushing Simon away. 'She just had too much to drink. Maybe she's not used to it. I'll take her home.'

'Right so. Whatever,' said Simon, heading back to the group.

'There was a girl here, I swear!' I didn't understand why neither of them would believe me.

'OK, Jacki, just take it easy. We're going home now.' He helped me to my feet.

I shivered as we walked along the path, the chill seeping through my skin. I had tried to explain to Colin that I wasn't out of it, that I had seen a girl in the trees, but he was having none of it. The night had got even darker, a half-moon offering the only light from a starless sky. I pulled the baggy shirt tightly around me. Colin noticed and immediately offered me his jacket.

'No, I can't be taking all your clothes.'

'I insist.'

I put on his jacket and instantly warmed up. Even though I was freaked out by what had just happened, I felt safe with Colin. He seemed to know every pothole and every protruding branch on that path. I stayed close behind him, mirroring his every move, so I wouldn't trip over.

'Tonight was fun. Thanks for inviting me up to the forest,'

I said, trying to forget about the girl. Was she just some strange hallucination? She had looked very real. Maybe I'd just had one drink too many as Colin thought. But Dr Cahill's words kept coming into my mind: *something supernatural*.

'So, do you like Simon?' said Colin.

'Oh . . . no. He's all right, I guess. But he's not . . .'

'Not Nick?' he suggested.

'What? How did you –'

'Doesn't take a genius to work that one out. Just be careful Jacki, he can be a bit of a dickhead.'

'What do you mean?' Part of me didn't want to know what he'd done in the past.

'He's just not very dependable. That's all. I suppose he's all right though, if you like the brooding handsome type.' Nick was kind of quiet, and I guess that could come across as moody, but I found it strangely attractive for some reason. Colin was probably just looking out for me, not wanting me to get my hopes up. But it was too late for that.

When we reached the top of my lane I began to take off Colin's jacket.

'Keep it for tonight,' he said.

'There's no need, honestly, sure I'm home now,' I said, nodding in the direction of the caravan.

'Well, OK. I'll see you tomorrow, if you're up to it.' He smiled at me as he put his jacket back on.

'Colin, I'm not even that drunk!'

'OK. And I'm not even that gay,' he replied, then turned and headed back down the lane.

I stood there until Colin had been absorbed into the darkness, and I could no longer hear his footsteps. I sat down on the strip of grass beside our hedge and rested my head in my hands. Great, now most of my new friends thought I was on drugs, and Colin thought I was a complete lightweight. Probably every one of them thought I was very strange. I didn't want to go inside. I didn't want Mum to ask me how my night went. I didn't want to lie down. I didn't want to go to sleep. A song circled round in my head. The rhyme I'd heard the little girl singing in the hall earlier.

> *Miss Jane had a bag*
> *And a mouse was in it.*
> *She opened the bag;*
> *He was out in a minute.*

Chapter 10

I slept in late the next morning – Mum had already left to meet the kitchen guy. I didn't feel well at all. I made an empty promise to myself never to drink again, then put on some make-up. My eyes still looked tired. The recurring nightmare had become such a guaranteed part of my routine that I wasn't even surprised when I'd woken up with a jolt, shaking and sweating. The nightmare was so strange. It was such a relief to wake up.

I ate a bowl of cereal and put on the least creased outfit from my suitcase – a short vintage floral dress and blue cardigan. Every time I opened the suitcase I felt guilty. I knew Alf's open letter was hidden in my shoebox. I tried not to feel too bad though. It wasn't like it was important . . . I'm sure he could do without a creepy note telling him to keep his mouth shut. But then I remembered reading somewhere that it was an actual crime to open someone else's post. And if Mum found out she'd freak; she was really particular about that sort of stuff. I rummaged beneath the clothes and took the letter out. I was going to tear it up. I held it in my hands, and prepared to rip. But then something told me not to. It's hard to describe, but I just had this feeling that something bad might happen if I did.

So I put it back underneath the clothes and snapped the suitcase shut.

Mum had left a pink Post-it note on the fridge saying she wouldn't be back until late. I didn't feel like spending the afternoon alone, so I grabbed my bag and headed for the café. I still felt kind of sleepy as I walked along, listening to Thin Lizzy on my iPod. But there was a nice breeze in the air, so I'd completely woken up by the time I reached the café. An old-fashioned bicycle stood outside, with a basketful of flowers and a sign with the words CUPCAKE CAFÉ in bold pink lettering. I peered in the window. A woman was busy arranging a display of cupcakes on the counter. She spotted me, unlocked the door and ushered me inside.

'Hello,' she said. 'Lovely day, isn't it?' She wore a badge with the name ALI attached to her apron with a little daisy pin. I guessed she was about fifty. She had a pretty oval face and her hair was tied up in a messy bun.

'So you're open again?' I said.

'We are indeed,' replied Ali, placing the final cupcake on to the stand. The little cakes had icing in assorted pastel colours; some had sprinkles and some had little edible butterflies on top. The Cupcake Café was one of the cutest places I'd ever seen. The walls were covered with pale pink polka dots, there were white tables with pretty placemats and chairs with pink cushions. Fairy lights were draped around the pillars at the counter and jam jars with little candles were scattered around the place.

I picked up a menu and read through it.

'What can I get you?' Ali asked. 'We have a nice selection of teas and smoothies and pastries. And of course our famous cupcakes.'

'I'll have a strawberry tea. And a pink cupcake,' I said. 'And can I use a computer?'

'Go ahead, use whichever one you like. Will I wait a while before I serve your tea?'

'Thanks, yeah, just need a few minutes,' I said.

There was a long table by the wall with three white Macs sitting on it. I sat down in front of the one nearest the window.

I messaged Hannah, Sophie and Ross, letting them know that things were looking up in Avarna, but didn't tell them about any of the weird episodes. I told them all about Nick and Colin and the others I'd met up in the forest. I didn't mention the girl in the trees though. I had pushed that whole experience to the back of my mind. After I'd messaged them I messed around on the Internet for a bit. I read through a couple of blog posts. Then I typed Beth Cullen into the search box. Even though I didn't like thinking about what had happened to her, I couldn't help wanting to know more. The first result was an article from the *Irish Times*, about Beth and three other women whose murders remained unsolved.

Following an extensive search, Beth Cullen's body was found close to the Avarna mines in Co. Leitrim in late December 1986. Gardai investigating the murder questioned a number of suspects, but no one was charged. Twenty-two-year-old Ms Cullen had been shopping for Christmas presents in Carrick-on-Shannon and had been sighted cycling just outside the town at around 4.30 p.m. on 21st December. Her parents raised the alarm when she did not return home for dinner that evening. Her bicycle was recovered three miles from where her body was found . . .

'Hi, Jacki,' said a voice from behind. I closed the tab and turned round. Emily was standing there, looking like a mini-rainbow in a polka-dot skirt, a stripy coloured T-shirt and purple Nikes.

'One chocolate cupcake, please, Ali,' she said, and then propped herself on the chair beside me.

'What you up to?' she asked, logging into the computer next to mine.

'Nothing much,' I said, clearing the search history with two swift clicks.

She looked even prettier in daylight. Her hair was a stunning dark red and she had a perfect button nose. She was smaller than me, maybe about five foot, and her nails were painted bright blue.

'Anything interesting happen after we left last night?' I said.

'Nope, not really. I went home pretty soon afterwards.' If she knew about my freak-out, she didn't say anything.

'Have you heard from Nick?' I asked. I wondered how he was doing. And how long it would take him to get over Sarah . . .

'No, I texted him, but he didn't reply. Nobody's heard from him yet. Poor guy. And he goes to the same school as her and everything. I'm so glad I go to an all-girls school. No fear of bumping into any ex-boyfriends.'

'You go to St Mary's?' I said, noticing the transition-year pin on her bag.

'Yep, I'm going into fifth year. Are you going there?'

'Yeah, I'm going into transition year. I'm glad you'll be there. At least now I'll know one person.' I was so relieved. Knowing just one person, even if they were in a different year to me, made the thought of the first day at school slightly less terrifying.

'St Mary's is actually an all-right place. I think you'll like it.

I'll introduce you to lots of people, don't worry. Put your number in there,' said Emily, handing me her phone, which was decorated with purple diamanté studs.

I put my name in, followed by a smiley face. I really was in a good mood now that school was a less intimidating prospect. I didn't think I'd ever feel OK about the uniform though. Wine was so not my colour.

I noticed one new email. It was a friend request from Emily. I turned and smiled at her.

'We're officially friends now,' she said jokingly.

Ali brought over the tea and cupcakes. We moved away from the computers and sat down at one of the tables. A few minutes later I noticed a dark-haired guy with glasses outside approaching the café door. He seemed to spot Emily and stepped back to check his reflection in the glass. When he saw me looking he stopped fixing his hair and opened the door.

'David!' said Emily. 'You're back!' She got up and rushed over to the door to give him a hug. 'How was your trip?'

'Hi, Emily,' he replied, blushing slightly from her embrace. 'It was brilliant. Really cool.'

I remembered Nick and Colin had mentioned David at the table quiz. He had braces and was about a foot taller than Emily. From his reaction to her hug I guessed he was one of her many admirers.

'David, this is Jacki,' said Emily, grabbing his arm and bringing him over to the table.

'Hi,' said David, sitting down beside Emily. 'Nice to meet you.'

'I just moved here,' I said. 'A few weeks ago.'

'Yeah, I heard,' said David. 'Nick told me about you.'

Now it was my turn to blush. *Nick told him about me*. So Nick had been talking about me. Which meant Nick was thinking about me. I wanted to ask him what Nick had said. I wanted to ask him to repeat every single syllable exactly as he'd heard it, but I decided to keep quiet and hope no one could see my delight.

'You had fun in Japan then?' said Emily.

'It was epic. I have Colin's stuff here,' he said, putting a plastic bag with some Japanese lettering on it on the table. 'And I got you something,' he added, rummaging through its contents. He pulled out a little Hello Kitty purse and gave it to Emily.

'Aww, wow! Thanks!'

'And you can have Sarah's one,' he said to me.

'Oh . . . I don't think I –'

'No, it's no problem – have it. I'm so glad I don't have to pretend to like that girl any more.' David handed me the purse. I said thanks, but felt awkward taking it from him. David told us more about his holiday, and then he and Emily started to gossip about people I didn't know. My mind began to wander. I thought about Beth again. How could somebody just vanish? Especially in a little village? How could she be cycling home one minute, and be gone the next? But when I thought of her I didn't imagine her cycling along the road. I thought of her pale frozen body lying on the ground. I hated that image. It was really detailed and horribly clear. I gripped the plastic purse so tightly that it left an imprint in my palm.

'Here's Nick,' whispered Emily.

I looked up to see him trudging along the path outside. I put the purse in my bag and banished the image of Beth from my mind. Nick spotted us inside and pushed open the door. He looked tired as he came over to the table. Tired and grumpy. But still very hot.

'We heard what happened . . .' said Emily sympathetically. 'How are you feeling?'

'I don't want to talk about it,' he said, sitting across from me.

Nick proceeded to eat four cupcakes and ignored Emily's advice that comfort eating would solve nothing. I wanted to say something to him, but was afraid I'd say the wrong thing. I didn't want to mess up my chances.

Shortly afterwards Colin came into the café, and almost dived for the bag when he saw it on the table. His face lit up as he pulled out the DVDs and Manga stuff. 'David, you're an absolute legend,' he said. 'I love you.'

'Steady now,' said David.

Colin smiled as he flicked through one of the books. I'm not sure if I've ever seen anyone look so happy. It reminded me of Mum when she'd found our Italian kitchen tiles at half price.

'Fancy going to Sligo later?' said Nick. 'I need to get away from here.'

I'd have done anything to go to Sligo with Nick, but I didn't want to sound too keen, so I waited to see what the others would say.

'Can't,' said David. 'My parents had to go off to Wexford for the night and they forgot to leave me money.'

'So you have a free gaff?' asked Nick, his voice more animated.

A look of horror spread across David's face. 'Nick, I'm not ~ving another party. You know the shit I got into after the last

'Not a party, David . . . just a few friends over.' Nick had already got his phone out and was busy texting.

'Fine,' said David. 'But you're not allowed to bring any of your bandmates.'

'But –'

'I mean it.'

'OK!' said Nick.

'Relax, David,' said Emily. 'It'll be fun.'

'So you're coming then, yeah?' he said, sitting back in his seat.

'Definitely. And Jacki will come, won't you?' She smiled at me.

'Yeah, OK,' I said. A party would be the perfect place to talk to Nick.

'And can I bring a few of the girls?' Emily suggested.

'Sure.'

'So she gets to bring people and I don't?' Nick protested.

'Nick, at my last party your bassist *ate* my goldfish.'

'That was so funny,' said Nick with a laugh.

'It was *not* funny. It was traumatic,' said David.

I was so excited. I couldn't wait for the party. This was even better than a trip to Sligo. This was a house party. With no parents. Maybe something would happen with Nick. I knew it was a long shot, because he had just broken up with his girlfriend, but that didn't stop me imagining. I just wished my excitement wasn't dampened by the sick feeling in my stomach. I had begun to feel very ill again, just like I had the night before in the forest and the other night in my back garden.

I looked around for the bathroom and made my way to the back of the café.

'It's kind of dark in there,' said Ali as I walked past the counter. 'I haven't had a chance to change the light bulb yet.'

'That's OK,' I said, pushing open the bathroom door. It was a little room painted dark green and there was a tiny window up high on the back wall that didn't let much light in. The toilet was old, with a wooden seat, and a chain dangled from the cast-iron cistern hanging up on the wall.

As I washed my hands I stared into the mirror above the basin. My eyeliner had smudged, and dark shadows hung under my eyes. I reapplied my make-up and fixed my hair, trying to make myself feel better. I needed to go to that party. I was already planning my outfit, trying to remember what clothes were clean. I put my make-up back in my bag and tried to turn the key in the lock, but it wouldn't open. It was one of those old ones that you had to twiddle a bit. I tried the lock again. It still wouldn't budge. There was probably a knack to it . . . I could just call out for Ali to help me. But that would be embarrassing.

Eventually the key turned. As I pushed open the door I felt something rush past me. Something familiar. A dark figure with flowing black hair. It disappeared so quickly that it became little more than a blur.

My heart thumped rapidly. I tried to convince myself that it was nothing, but deep down inside I knew I needed to accept that something strange was going on. Had I just seen a *ghost*? It was a crazy thought; I didn't believe in that kind of thing. Or did I? My brain was telling me not to be ridiculous, but my body was reacting so strongly: my legs felt wobbly and my hands were clammy. After what had happened in the garden, then the forest last night . . . and now this . . . What was going on? I thought back to the card Dr Cahill had given me for the healer. Maybe it was worth asking him a few questions. But I quickly dismissed this idea. There had to be a simple explanation. It was probably stress, or tiredness . . .

I forced myself to calm down. I took a few slow deep breaths and waited until I felt normal enough to face the others.

Later that evening Colin came over to the caravan so we could go to the party together. I wasn't sure where Mum was, but I knew she wouldn't be happy about the mess. There were clothes scattered everywhere. I had no time to clean up – I was far too busy trying to make myself look as irresistible as possible. Colin enjoyed trying on various items from my wardrobe as I got ready. I needed to find something perfect to wear. I rummaged through my suitcase and pulled out my tight white shirt.

'Colin, that's not going to fit you!' I said as he tried to squeeze himself into my denim waistcoat. To my disbelief he managed it.

'Do I look like Kate Moss?' he asked.

'Spitting image,' I giggled, as I searched for my other ankle boot. It was impossible to find anything.

'We should put on some music,' said Colin. He grabbed my iPod and within seconds 'Girls Just Wanna Have Fun' was blasting from the portable speakers. Colin tied my red silk scarf round his neck and proceeded to dance around the tiny caravan.

'Don't look,' I said as I changed into my shirt and tartan skirt.

'What you're sellin' I ain't buyin',' said Colin, mid twirl.

I put on a silver necklace and my leather jacket. My outfit was finally coming together.

'Lookin' good,' said Colin.

The door swung open and almost hit him in the back. Oh no, here we go, I was going to be in major trouble. The caravan was in a state.

'Hi, Mum, I was just about to clean this —'

'Don't worry about it,' she said, struggling in with shopping bags. Colin grabbed them for her and found a clear space on the table.

'We're going to a party,' he explained, motioning to the piles of clothes. 'A girl has to look her best.'

Mum smiled. 'Jacki, it's fine. You go off to your party.' She started to unpack groceries and I put on the rest of my make-up in the bathroom while Colin chatted to her about house renovations. He was one of those guys who parents loved because he was so chatty and polite. I could tell from her tone of voice that Mum seemed to be in a really good mood. I filed a mental note to bring Colin round more often.

As I stepped out of the bathroom I heard a car outside. 'Who's that?' I asked, looking out the window.

'It's Des,' said Mum.

'It's half nine. Why is Des here?'

'We're going to the Chinese in Carrick.'

'What? Why?'

'He asked me if I wanted to —'

'Wait . . . is this *a date*?' I asked, dreading her answer.

Colin stood awkwardly between the two of us, trapped in the tiny space.

'Yes. It's a date.' She knew I wouldn't explode with Colin there. I couldn't believe it. She was actually going on a date with him. He was totally not right for her. This was ridiculous.

'Here,' she said, handing me twenty euro. 'Don't be back too late.'

'*You* don't be back too late!' I shrieked.

Mum smiled and despite my effort to pull away, she kissed me on the cheek. 'Have a nice night,' she said.

'You too,' said Colin as she left the caravan. He turned to me and shrugged. 'She seems happy.'

I hated to admit that he was right. I felt disloyal to my dad, even though I knew it was unfair. 'I wish we had some vodka,' I said.

'Whoa there,' said Colin. 'Don't want you hallucinating again.'

'I didn't hallucinate,' I said. 'There was somebody in those trees.'

'Maybe you saw a ghost!' said Colin. 'There's rumours that those woods are haunted.'

I thought back to the bathroom at the café. 'I didn't see a ghost. She was . . . she . . . I don't know. But I didn't see a ghost. There's no such thing.' It sounded convincing when I said it aloud.

'Is so,' said Colin, whooshing me out of the caravan.

'No, there's not,' I said, locking the door behind us. 'When you die you are dead – that's it. You rot into nothing and you are never coming back.'

'Whatever you say,' Colin replied. 'Now, let's get ready to party!'

Chapter 11

'Right, guys, you can do whatever you like, just don't move anything, don't break anything and don't get sick on anything,' said David Mulvey as he dropped a bag of tortilla chips on to the mahogany coffee table. From the leather couch, I looked around the enormous sitting room. It resembled a small ball-room, with its dark red walls, smooth wooden floor and crystal chandelier suspended from the high ceiling. The décor was surely the work of an interior designer. It was wonderfully elaborate and everything matched perfectly. His house was probably the biggest in Avarna. On the walk down I'd learned from Colin that it had six bedrooms, three bathrooms, a Jacuzzi in the basement and a tennis court out the back. I carefully lifted my can of cider, terrified of spilling it. I now understood why David had been reluctant to have a party. There were so many things that could get broken.

Nick was slouched in an armchair. His head was resting against one of his hands and he was staring at the TV in a kind of trance. He looked hotter than ever in a white Undertones T-shirt. Colin sat cross-legged on the red rug on the floor, his fingers clasping a game controller and his eyes fixed on the plasma screen. His opponent, Simon, knelt beside him. He seemed to think that the way he manoeuvred his tongue affected his performance, as he stuck it out to the side every time his virtual car came to a bend.

Chris was sitting next to me on the sofa. He was wearing a big black hoodie and seemed to be engrossed in the game. His brother, Pete, sat on the other end of the couch. He was a good-looking guy, probably about sixteen, with a piercing on his left eyebrow. He'd been texting constantly since his arrival. Fitz sat in an armchair in the corner rolling a spliff. This wasn't exactly the crazy house party they'd predicted. But I guess it was pretty early.

'When is Emily getting here?' I asked.

'Soon . . . I think,' said David. He sounded nervous.

'Do us a favour and go for it this time, will you?' said Colin.

David looked embarrassed. 'Yes, I will . . . probably,' he said.

'Shouldn't be too hard,' said Simon. 'Everyone knows she's easy.'

'Hey!' I shouted, not wanting to let him get away with that remark.

'OH YEAH!' exclaimed Colin as his car sped over the finish line in front of Simon's.

'Carla, I thought you were going out,' said David as his fourteen-year-old sister came into the room. She had jet-black hair and was wearing a black corset dress and lots of eye make-up.

'Nah, I thought this would be way more interesting.'

'You're so annoying,' said David through gritted teeth.

'Oh, and I invited Amanda over,' added Carla, with a mischievous grin.

'You know I hate that girl!' said David. 'You totally just did that to piss me off.'

Carla shrugged and walked out of the sitting room. David scrunched up his fists and took a deep breath, trying to calm himself down.

'This party needs some tunes,' said Chris, getting out of his seat. He went over to the CD player next to me and began to check out David's parents' extensive music collection. Rory Gallagher was soon thundering out of the surround sound system. I loved Rory Gallagher; I had all his albums. I leaned over and scanned the rest of the collection. There was some U2, the Stones, the Cranberries. David's parents had good taste.

'Right, who wants to challenge the champion?' asked Colin, dangling the spare controller above his head.

'Go on then,' said Fitz, handing his spliff to Chris. Nick hadn't spoken one word in the last ten minutes. I watched him get up from his chair and walk out to the kitchen. The doorbell rang and David scurried to answer it.

Emily came into the sitting room, wearing a stunning short blue dress. She sat down on the couch next to me. David was wandering around looking nervous. For a moment it looked as if he was going to sit beside her, but then he turned round and hurried out the door. I wanted to talk to Nick, but the right time never seemed to arrive. I'd only sat on the couch to be in the same room as him.

'I love your eye shadow, Emily,' I said, trying to think about something else. It was dark blue and glittery, and matched her eyes. She looked very pretty.

'Oh, thanks . . . I got it for my birthday.'

'Do you want a drink?' I asked her.

'No, thanks, I don't drink. I'll have a few of those crisps though,' she said, leaning over to get some from the bag on the table.

'Where did David go?' I asked.

'Dunno, he was acting kind of weird,' said Emily.

I smirked and nudged her. 'That's 'cause he's really into you,' I teased.

'*What?* No, he's not!' she said, but I could tell she was happy to hear it.

'Yeah, he is,' Colin piped up. 'Put him out of his misery, will you?'

I really liked that Colin could be so direct and friendly at the same time. And Emily seemed to be taking it well. I smiled to myself. I was beginning to feel comfortable with this group of new friends.

By eleven o'clock David's fears had been realized. Most of the surrounding area's teenage population had descended on the house. But he was concentrating so hard on impressing Emily that he didn't have time to worry. So I started to worry for him. It's not like I had anything better to do – I'd hardly seen Nick all night. I was starting to think that maybe he was avoiding me. He obviously wasn't that interested after all. I convinced Chris that seeing if he could lift a plasma screen television with one hand wasn't a good idea and I managed to direct a brown-haired girl to the bathroom before her beer came up to meet the carpet.

'Jacki! Don't worry about it,' said Colin, as I tried to wrestle a crystal clock from Simon. I gave up and flopped down on the couch.

'Here, put on something good,' said a guy wearing a baseball cap in the corner.

'What did you say?' said Fitz.

'I said put on something good!' the guy shouted.

'Do you know who this is?' said Fitz, walking slowly towards him.

'Eh . . . no.' The guy looked kind of scared.

'This is Rory Gallagher. An absolute legend. How dare you!'

'Oh, right . . . sorry, man . . . It's just this album has been on for ages.' He was right – nobody had bothered to put on something different. I usually delighted in being the DJ, but I'd been too preoccupied with making sure David's house didn't get trashed.

'Right, fine,' said Fitz. 'I'll change it . . . any requests?'

'Do they have any Thin Lizzy?' asked Colin.

'Think so,' I said.

Colin gave me a wink as the intro to 'Dancing in the Moonlight' came on.

'Ah, deadly!' said David as he and Emily came into the sitting room.

'Come on,' shouted Colin, jumping up and holding out his hand.

'No, it's OK,' I said. I wasn't in the mood for dancing. I'd really thought something might happen between me and Nick, but that was looking unlikely now.

'Jacki, don't make me dance by myself!'

'I don't really feel like –'

'Come on!' Colin grabbed my hand and pulled me up. I gave in and danced with him. By the second verse almost everybody was up dancing and singing along, and for one tiny moment I didn't care where Nick was.

When the song finished I sat down on the couch and Colin went to get us drinks. My eyes met those of Carla's friend, Amanda, who was hovering awkwardly in the middle of the room.

'Do you want to sit down?' I asked her.

Turned out I was really going to regret that. She talked at me non-stop for ten minutes: '. . . we met at this random party and got on great and everything, and we made out for a while, but then the next week . . . he told me he loved me. I thought that was a bit weird. I mean, we'd been seeing each other for, like, a week. Don't you find that weird? So obviously I said, "OK, thanks," or whatever and then dumped him the next day by text. But anyway, yeah, that was him texting me there. He's been practically stalking me ever since. Carla says to just ignore him and he'll get bored with it, but it's totally freaking me out. What if he gets obsessed with me or something?' Amanda took a sip from her drink. I'd been listening to her love-life dilemmas for far too long. She'd gone into way too much detail and unfortunately I was trapped. Emily was nowhere to be seen, and some guy had nabbed Colin to fix the DVD player. And there was still no sign of Nick.

'So . . . how do you know Carla?' I said, eager to steer the conversation away from Amanda's more personal activities.

'I met her at Irish College last year and we stayed friends. She's so nice. I haven't seen much of her tonight though. She's been with some guy most of the time. Do you have a boyfriend?'

'No.'

'Yeah, me neither. I'm enjoying it. It's weird, 'cause I'm

hardly ever single.' Amanda tossed her hair over her shoulder. 'So, think any of the guys here tonight are cute?' she asked.

I looked around the room. Colin was kneeling on the floor in front of the television, with a guy whose name I couldn't remember standing beside him. Chris was jumping on the table, chewing on a mouthful of nachos. Simon sat on the other couch, beside two pale-faced guys in the middle of an arm-wrestle.

'Eh . . . no,' I said.

'That one's kinda hot,' she said, pointing over at Colin.

'Oh, I wouldn't say you'd have much luck with him,' I said.

'Tried, have you? I reckon I could get in there. No offence.'

'Oh, none taken . . . I think you should definitely go for it then. His name is Colin. Excuse me, I just have to go and find my friend.'

I escaped to look for Emily and I found her pressed up against the wall, with David kissing her neck and running his hands through her hair. I was happy for them, but couldn't help feeling down and a little envious at the same time. I just wished me and Nick were talking, let alone kissing. Life was just so unfair sometimes. I decided it was time to go home. I walked quickly past them, and up the stairs. Colin had put my jacket and bag in one of the bedrooms to keep them safe. I opened a few doors before I found the master bedroom with the coats all sprawled out on the bed. I spotted my leather jacket easily but couldn't see my handbag anywhere. I'd begun to rummage through the coats when I heard somebody come in behind me. I turned round and to my complete surprise saw Nick slamming the door shut and locking it.

'Hi,' I said.

He jumped with fright. 'Oh, Jacki, I didn't see you there.'

'What are you doing?' I said.

'Shhh,' he whispered. 'I'm hiding.'

I quickly checked my outfit to make sure I looked OK. I couldn't believe we were alone. I love how unbelievably perfect moments can just pounce on you sometimes. Especially when you've almost given up hope.

'Who from?' I asked.

'Nick!' shouted a girl's voice from the hall.

'Is that Amanda?' I said quietly.

'You know her?'

'Just met her. She's a bit annoying.' I was so glad Nick had locked the door. I couldn't bear it if Amanda barged in and ruined our moment alone. I wondered if my make-up had worn off. It was pretty dark though, only the bedside lamps were on, so he probably wouldn't notice.

'She's insane. The lads thought it would be funny to tell her that I fancied her. I'm going to kill them.'

'She is very pretty.'

'But she's actually crazy. That cancels it out.'

Nick stepped away from the door. 'What are you doing in here anyway? You're not going, are you?'

'Oh no . . . I was just, just getting something from my bag. I left it up here with my jacket.'

He sat down on the bed beside me. My eyes rested on the curls at the back of his neck. I breathed in his aftershave and felt a little shock when his leg touched mine.

'I may never be able to leave this room,' he whispered.

That's OK by me, I thought to myself, my heart starting to thump.

'I've hardly got to talk to you at all tonight,' he said. 'I've been trying to avoid that girl and she always seemed to be in the same room as you.' So he hadn't been ignoring me after all. It was such a relief to know that. Why did I always think the worst when it came to boys?

'Did you want to talk to me about something?' I asked.

'Well, no, not really anything in particular, just, you know, chat.' Nick pulled at a thread hanging from his torn denims.

'OK,' I said.

'Sorry, I'm terrible at this.'

'At what?'

'Talking to girls who I like.' He looked up at me.

That was it. I was officially in love.

Neither of us said anything for a moment. Then I moved a little closer. And he leaned forward and kissed me. In that moment nothing else in my life mattered. Anything that had gone before was just leading up to that soft, flawless kiss.

Nick gently pushed me back on the bed. We kissed again, more intense this time. I shivered slightly, a little bit from nerves, but mostly from excitement. It felt amazing. His hand brushed against my neck, and with each touch I became more lost in the moment. This incredible, magical moment. It was definitely my version of heaven. For a few seconds it was perfect. But then suddenly and for no reason I began to feel weird and everything changed. The atmosphere, the mood, everything. I could hear my own voice as if it didn't belong to me; it sounded different: scared and nasty.

'Get off me!' I could hear myself saying.

'What?' said Nick.

'Stop. Stop it!'

Nick backed away.

'OK, OK, just calm dow—'

I could hear Nick's confusion, but I couldn't calm down – I was in pure panic.

'Get *off* me!'

'Jacki, I'm not on you! Will you stop shouting?'

I could hear him speak but I couldn't answer. I felt as if I was no longer lying on the bed in the master bedroom. I was lying on a damp carpet of twigs and leaves out under a black sky, with a brutal, heavy body pushing down on me, and a sweaty hand groping the inside of my legs. I tried to push him away but he was much too strong. The body pushed down on me, harder and harder.

'Is everything OK in there?' shouted Colin from the other side of the door.

'Yes.' Nick's voice was shaking. 'Yes, every—'

'Get off me! Get off! No, stop it, *stop it*!'

'Jacki? Is that you?' said Colin.

'Get off me!'

'Jacki, I'm not near you!' said Nick. 'Please stop. You're scaring me. Please just calm —'

'Get off me!'

The door rattled on its hinges as Colin slammed against it.

'Nick, open this door *now*,' he shouted.

'Wait, just wait.' Nick scurried off the bed.

There was a loud bang on the door.

The door rattled again. But it didn't budge.

'Jacki . . . listen to me,' said Nick. 'What the *hell* is wrong with you?' He ran over to the door and tried to open the lock, but the key went tumbling to the floor.

'For God's sake,' he mumbled.

There was another loud bang. The door swung open, hitting Nick hard in the face. He let out a howl of pain.

'Jacki!' Colin could see me jerking about on the bed, desperately trying to wrestle with the invisible attacker. 'What did you do to her?'

I could still hear everything that Colin and Nick were saying. They couldn't see my attacker, and I could only feel him.

'I did NOTHING. I didn't touch her!' shouted Nick. Colin gave him a questioning look.

'OK, we were just . . . well . . . you know . . . She wanted to! And then she just totally freaked!'

By this time a group of partiers were huddled at the door, all staring at me. Colin slammed it shut, abruptly blocking their view. Then he sat down on the bed and leaned over me.

"Get off me!' I shouted.

'Jacki,' he said. Colin grabbed my wrist and this suddenly brought me back. I was back in reality, shivering uncontrollably.

'I have to go,' I said, sitting up. 'I . . . I have to go now.' I threw the coats off the bed until I found my bag, then ran from the room towards the stairs.

'Jacki, where are you going?' shouted Nick.

'Home. I'm sorry. I have to get out of here now.' I didn't understand what had just happened, but I knew I needed to get away.

I rushed down the stairs and out the front door. Colin came running after me.

'Jacki, wait. You can't go by yourself. Wait there, I'll get your jacket.' Colin hurried back into the house.

I stared at my reflection in the passenger window of a car in the driveway. I was horribly pale. A burning sensation ripped through my skull. Things were getting out of hand. What had happened in that room was far worse than any headache or nightmare or vision. I knew what I needed to do. I needed to visit the healer as soon as possible. I might have refused to believe in that sort of stuff, but now I was desperate. I couldn't deny it: something supernatural was happening.

That night I lay in my bed, trying to fight back the tears. My chances with Nick had been completely ruined. I'd been so close to him. We could have kissed more . . . and then he might have asked me on a date. But I'd ruined it. I'd ruined everything. Or rather *something* had ruined everything. Was it really something supernatural, whatever that might mean? I wished it was morning so I could ring Ger Rapple's number.

When you die you are dead – that's it. You rot into nothing and you are never coming back . . . Right?

Chapter 12

I woke up late for the second day in a row and noticed a big purple bruise on my elbow. I reckoned I must have whacked it off the bedpost at David's, but then again the bruise did look like it was a few days old. Maybe it had been there for a while and I just hadn't seen it. The headache was back, worse than ever. I had dozed off around 6 a.m. and despite being exhausted I had started to dream. I didn't dream about the drunk man and the angry driver and the brown leather bag. I dreamed about lying on a damp carpet of twigs with a heavy body pressing down on me and hands groping me. It was like what I'd felt at David's. But this dream was even more terrifying than the other one. In this dream I wasn't just an observer; I was a participant. An unwilling one. I don't scare easily, but I couldn't help feeling frightened now. The dream was so real I felt like I had actually been attacked. Even after I'd woken up I couldn't shake off the terror I felt inside. And when I'd been on the bed I *had* been awake. Flashbacks from last night kept coming into my mind, the most heart-wrenching one being the look of confusion on Nick's face. I couldn't think about him now though. I had to get going.

I got out of bed, went into our tiny bathroom and turned

on the shower. As I took off my pyjamas my heart started to beat faster and faster. There was another bruise, and another and another. My body was covered in them. Big black dirty bruises, all along my shoulders and chest and thighs. The one on my neck was so dark I couldn't see my heart-shaped freckle. I was about to scream but stopped myself. Mum didn't need to know about this. She would freak out and drag me straight to the doctor. I was so frightened, but I desperately tried to calm down. I had a quick shower, shivering even though the water was scorching hot. My mind raced, trying to find a logical explanation for these marks on my skin. They hadn't been there when I was getting ready for bed. Surely if I'd been thrashing around in my sleep Mum would have woken up and stopped me? Maybe they weren't bruises . . . they didn't hurt at all . . . maybe they were just stains of some sort. I scrubbed at one on my shoulder but it didn't budge. What the hell was happening to me? I was on the verge of tears but I held it together. I needed to get to the healer's house.

I dressed quickly, throwing on anything I could find. Mum wasn't anywhere near the house so I left her a note saying I'd be back in a couple of hours. Then I ran up towards the mines until I could get enough coverage, my blue Doc Martens splashing in last night's puddles, spattering rainwater on to my denims. I took the card from my pocket and dialled the number.

'Hello?' A woman's voice answered.

'Hello,' I said. 'Um, I was given Ger Rapple's number and I need to see him urgently. Today.'

'I'm sorry, dear, but he's fully booked today. And I'm afraid he's busy for the next two weeks. But I can make you an appointment for then.'

My heart sank and tears sprang into my eyes. I couldn't help it. 'Please,' I said, my voice shaking. 'This is an emergency. Dr Cahill said this might be the answer to some . . . headaches I've been having. They're getting worse and I can't sleep. Please help me,' I begged, no longer caring if I sounded desperate.

'OK, dear, just calm down. Do you think you can get here in the next ten minutes? He's just had a cancellation. If you can, then I'll ask if he can see you.'

'Yes, that's fine. I'll be there.'

'OK, now, can you give me some details.'

I gave her my name, address and date of birth, then rooted around in my bag for a piece of paper and scribbled the directions on the back of my Cupcake Café receipt.

Ger Rapple's house was on the side of a mountain, about a twenty-minute walk from the mines. To make it I'd have to run the whole way there. I didn't hesitate. It was uphill all the way, but I kept running. My stomach churned and my head thumped with every heavy step, but I had to keep on going, I had no choice. The sun blasted down on the road and I squinted, searching for Ger Rapple's house in the distance. I wasn't familiar with this part of Avarna; the scenery was all new to me. To my right was a narrow field covered with overgrown grass and chunks of rotting bark and on the far side of this field stood a forest of tall conifers, their tips piercing the pale blue sky. To my left the view was breathtaking. A huge green expanse led down to a vast lake, its surface glittering in the sunlight. On the lake's shore stood the majestic ruins of a castle, its outer walls still intact and dotted with glassless arched windows. This part of Avarna was incredibly beautiful. I could see the healer's house not too far away, so I picked up my pace and kept going.

I tried not to think about Nick. But I just couldn't stop myself picturing him. Last night had been so perfect and I had completely messed it up. I wanted to rewind to yesterday. When it comes to love sometimes I think the lead-up is the best part. Yes, it's erratic and uncertain, but at least there is nothing to lose. Once you finally get the person you want, then comes the horrible possibility of losing them. I had won Nick and lost him all in one night. I really couldn't dwell on that now though. Besides the fact that it made me ache inside, I had something much more urgent to worry about.

The two-storey stone house had a red front door and a balcony that looked out on the magnificent view. To the right, beyond a colourful garden, stood a wooden log cabin, a wind chime on its porch tinkling in the light breeze. For a split second I thought about turning round. I thought about running back down the mountain and going back into the caravan, and getting back into bed, and forgetting any of this had ever happened. Part of me was tempted to do this. But another part of me knew that if I kept on ignoring whatever this was . . . something even worse might happen. And I didn't want to imagine what could be worse than last night. So I knocked on the door of the house and a man whom I assumed was Ger Rapple opened it. He was not at all as I'd expected. I had imagined he might look a bit strange, a touch wacky, but he was really normal. He wore a blue striped shirt and beige cords. He had broad shoulders, tanned skin and a short grey beard. I guessed he was about fifty, and he had a warm smile that was very welcoming. I instantly felt calmer.

'You must be Jacki,' he said. 'Nice to meet you.'

'Hi,' I said as I shook his hand. He had a calm air about him, completely relaxed and untroubled. I was starting to think that maybe everything was going to be OK after all. Ger would figure out what was wrong and my life would go back to the way it used to be.

'Is there anyone here with you?' he asked, looking down the driveway. 'When people are under eighteen I prefer that they have somebody with them.'

'No, there isn't . . . but I really need to see you. Today,' I insisted as politely as possible. I couldn't miss out on this, the possibility to switch my life back. There was no way I could explain this to Mum. I needed Ger to see me. I looked at him pleadingly.

He hesitated, but to my relief, said 'OK then, this way,' and I followed him over to the log cabin. It was really bright inside, the sunlight beaming in through the back window. A soothing violin concerto played on the stereo in the corner. 'OK, Jacki,' he said. 'What can I do for you?'

'Something very weird is happening to me,' I said. 'I need to know what's going on.'

The details came gushing out of me all at once. The nightmares, the visions, the headaches, the bruises and the mysterious attack. I told him about the girl I'd seen in the forest and in the café and about the dream I'd had last night. I didn't care if he thought I was crazy, I just needed to tell someone the whole story.

He didn't seem shocked by any of it. He simply looked at me for a few moments, as if deciding the best way to explain.

'OK,' he said. 'It seems to me that someone is trying to contact you.'

I had an idea what he was hinting at. But I needed to find out more.

'Who . . .?' I said.

'When I say "someone". . . I mean . . . someone from the other side.'

That's what I'd been afraid of.

'Like a . . . a ghost?' When I said it out loud I realized how utterly ridiculous it sounded.

'Yes, a spirit, perhaps. The headaches you described are a common side-effect of spirit contact.'

This was getting too much for me. After being so eager for answers, I wasn't prepared for it. I had to get out.

'I'd better go,' I said. 'I don't feel comfortable with all this.' I wasn't ready to hear it. I had let fear get the better of me. I'd been so frightened that I'd allowed myself to go beyond desperate. I should never have come here. *There's no such thing as ghosts*, I told myself. I had to get out of there. Ger did not stir, even as I made my way to the cabin door.

'I'm sorry,' I mumbled as I pushed the door open.

'Jacki?' he said.

I just wanted to leave. 'Yes?' I replied without looking back.

'Can I ask you a question?'

I hesitated, but turned round and nodded anyway, preparing to take off as soon as I had answered. Ger spoke quietly, so that I had to listen really closely to hear him. 'Your dad wants to know . . . why are you wearing his socks?'

I was suddenly aware of the feel of the thick grey cotton socks on my feet. They were my lucky socks. The ones that I wore when I had to do something I was nervous about. The ones I had taken from one of the plastic bin bags at the foot of

Mum's bed before she gave them away. That morning I'd put them on to try to make myself feel a bit better. Nobody knew I had them. Not even Mum. And there was absolutely no way Ger could have known or even guessed. I was wearing Doc Martens: my socks couldn't be seen. Besides, I hadn't even told him that my father was dead. I stood stuck to that spot for several moments.

'How did you . . . how did you know . . .?' My voice trailed off into nothing.

'Are you OK?' asked Ger.

'Yes. Yes, I'm fine.' I was desperately trying to hold back my tears, but failing miserably.

'Why don't you sit down.'

I walked back across the room and sat on one of the chairs. I felt like I was in a sort of trance. I couldn't feel my feet move; I was completely in shock.

'Here.' Ger gave me a tissue and I wiped my eyes.

'Are you . . . are you, like . . . talking to my dad?'

'We were only able to communicate for a few seconds. He's moved on, you see. He's at peace. Not like the spirit who's been trying to get in touch with you. She's not at peace. She needs your help to move on.'

I was so glad to hear that my dad's spirit was at peace, but disappointed that Ger couldn't talk to him for longer. I couldn't explain how he knew about the socks without accepting that what he was saying was true. Something or someone was trying to contact me. From the other side. I had no idea why they'd chosen me. I was a fifteen-year-old sceptic. Maybe Ger would know why.

'But why me?' I asked. 'Why is she contacting me? I've just moved here.'

'There must be a reason why she chose you,' said Ger. 'I'm not getting very many details about her . . . but I do think she had a violent death.'

'Was she . . . murdered?' I whispered.

'Perhaps.' Ger's voice was gentle. 'Jacki, some people are more in touch with the other side. I am, and so are you. She is contacting you through your dreams, and in other ways.'

I looked down at my bruised arm.

'Why would she . . . why would she do this to me?'

'She wanted to get your attention.'

'What's her name?' I asked, even though by now I had an idea what the answer might be.

'Jane.'

This name took me completely by surprise. I'd been expecting something else.

Ger saw my surprise. 'Does that mean anything to you?'

'Not at all. I thought it might have been a girl who was killed near my home . . . Beth Cullen. What . . . what does Jane want from me?'

'You have to figure that out on your own, I'm afraid. She chose you, not me.'

I guess it felt kind of an honour to be chosen, but at the same time I had no idea what on earth I could do. I wished she could find a less scary way to ask for help.

'How can I help her if I don't know what she wants?'

'You haven't been listening to her messages. Until today you didn't even think something like this was possible. You have to start listening. There must be links between the dreams you are having, the places you saw her.'

'If I listen, if I find out . . . will she go away?'

'Once this spirit gets help she'll move on. But . . .' Ger let his sentence trail off, and avoided looking at me. This worried me a bit.

'But what?' I said.

'Well . . . I wouldn't be surprised if something like this happens again in the future. It seems that a unique path has been chosen for you.'

I sighed as I imagined a lifetime of headaches and visions and nightmares.

'You can't ignore this any more. It's like driving along a road and completely disregarding the markings . . . eventually you're going to get hurt.'

More hurt than I already was? I could take the headaches and the nightmares, but last night had been unbearable. I didn't want to go through something like that again. Was Ger saying I had no choice? That I'd been chosen to do something, and that I had to accept whatever consequences came with it?

'What if I can't work it out?' I said. Just because I was prepared to accept that a spirit was contacting me, didn't mean I would suddenly get any better at figuring out what she wanted.

'You will. I know you will.'

Ger stood up and walked over to the bookshelf. He took down a small black book and handed it to me. MASTERING PSYCHIC PROTECTION was printed on the cover in tiny gold letters.

'I think you should read this,' he said.

'Is this to protect against the spirits?'

'Yes, but it will also help you learn how to defend yourself from people on this side. Here, the demand for the truth never quite matches up to the supply. Some spirits want to get their message across, but often there are people who don't want that message revealed.'

I took the book from him.

'You can choose to block this out, Jacki, choose to ignore it as you have been doing, but you do so at your own risk. If you don't start accepting who you are now, your health will just continue to get worse.'

Even though it was hard to believe, I was feeling better already.

'Thanks. I'm sorry for, well, you know . . . for being so rude earlier,' I said.

'It's fine,' he said. 'I understand. I'm not interested in trying to convert sceptics. People can believe whatever they want. And people can deny this stuff all they like . . . But as you know, when it's staring you in the face, it's very hard to get away from it.'

I felt guilty. Jane had been staring me straight in the face and I had explained her away. I tried to remember her features, but they were just a blur. Ger handed me another tissue and I wiped my face again. I'd been in such a rush that I'd forgotten to put on make-up and now must have looked a state, my bare face all red and puffy. The relief I felt meant that the tears just kept coming. I hardly ever cried; this was really not like me.

'How did you find out you had this ability?' I asked, trying to divert attention away from me as I pulled myself together.

'I sort of always knew I could do it. I just wasn't able to accept it. Or, rather, wasn't *willing* to accept it. It's not an easy thing to do, to acknowledge that you're different. I ignored it for years. I was very sick, in and out of hospital all the time. I'd been to see different doctors, but none of them seemed to be able to diagnose my condition. It baffled them. I went to a specialist in Dublin, and he said, "I think we both know what's wrong. You have a gift, and you're not using it." The specialist's grandfather was a healer too. He told me that the kind of healing I do can be traced right back to ancient Ireland. He gave me his grandfather's number, and it took off from there. I haven't been back to hospital since.'

'So what am I? I'm not a healer.'

'No. But you do have the ability to connect with spirits. You can be whatever you want to be, just as long as you remember to use your gift. You don't want to suppress it. You don't want to end up like I did.'

'Can you talk to my dad again?'

'I'm afraid not. I think your dad must have been worried about you. Maybe he needed you to believe what was going on. Communicating with spirits who are at rest is extremely difficult and can be highly dangerous. It should only be attempted in exceptional circumstances. That's not to say what you're about to embark on won't be dangerous as well.'

My stomach twisted. I wondered what else I'd have to endure.

'You can talk to people who are in between more easily,' said Ger. 'Spirits who haven't moved on. You can help them. You can help Jane.'

'How do I help her?'

'Just listen. Listen to what she has to say.'

Chapter 13

I walked back down the mountain in a kind of daze, replaying in my head everything Ger had said. I was grateful to have met him, and felt much better now that I knew there was an explanation. Not knowing had been scary. Last night had been one of the worst nights of my life. I'd been so freaked out – I'd never felt so out of control. But things were a bit better now because I understood what I had to do. In a strange way it was kind of exhilarating knowing I'd been chosen to do this. And having something to focus on distracted from the embarrassment of what had happened with Nick. I was going to help Jane. I was going to find out what had happened to her.

When I got back Mum was standing outside the front door of the house. She was talking to one of the builders, her gestures suggesting that she was unhappy about something. I knew those gestures well. I went inside the caravan and put the little black book that Ger had given me into the shoebox in the suitcase under my bed, right on top of Alf Meehan's letter. That suitcase was fast becoming a home for my top-secret stash. I wasn't used to keeping secrets from Mum. It wasn't like I told her everything, but I never kept anything major from her. I considered letting her in on my secret, but then decided against it. She had enough to worry about. She didn't need this too. Once I knew more, I'd tell her what was going on. Or I'd at least try. For now, I thought it was best to say nothing.

Ger had told me to listen. I was used to doing that. I was used to listening to songs, memorizing every word, repeating the particularly beautiful sentences and making note of why they worked so well. But it was hard to listen when you didn't know what you were supposed to be listening for. The clues were supposedly all around me, but how was I to know exactly where they were? I was too tired to concentrate now. My visit had been so overwhelming that I just wanted to rest for a bit. I thought I'd better say hi to Mum first though.

I tied my hair up in a ponytail and walked across the grass to the house. Mum had finished talking to the builder, and was now sifting through sheets of paper.

'Hi, Mum,' I said.

'Hello, stranger. Where have you been?' she asked. She seemed kind of flustered, but not at all suspicious.

'Oh . . . just around. The house is looking great, isn't it?' I stepped inside the hallway. It was starting to look like a home now. The walls were painted and the wooden floors were polished. I walked down the hall into the kitchen. There was so much more space than we'd had in Dublin. And everything was so new. I was beginning to get excited about moving in. The house really was gorgeous.

'Yes. It's looking great,' said Mum. 'But we have a problem.'

'What the hell is that smell?' I scrunched up my face in disgust, noticing it for the first time.

'That's the problem,' she said.

'What is it? It's horrible!' I covered my mouth and nose with my hand.

'You know how we had to dig up out the back for the new pipes?' she said, covering her nose too.

'Yes . . .' I vaguely remembered her complaining about it.

'There was a load of rubbish buried there. It absolutely stinks.'

'What kind of rubbish?'

'All sorts of stuff. Looks like Alf just buried his rubbish, rather than putting it in the bin.'

'Ew. Why would he do that?'

'No idea. Now we have to dig up the whole back garden and get rid of it. Just when I thought we were getting somewhere, something like this happens. I don't know if I'll ever get rid of that smell!'

Mum seemed very upset, and rightly so. I looked out the window.

There was a pile of horrible-looking rubbish: bursting plastic bags, rusting tins, torn packaging . . .

'Looks like he buried everything. God only knows what they're going to find down there.'

I suddenly thought of Jane. Maybe they were going to find a body. Maybe she was buried underneath the ground, having lain there for years. Maybe that's why she couldn't move on. I stared at the giant pile of rubbish. It might have polluted the air around it with a horrid stale smell, but potentially it held the answer to my mystery. I was getting ahead of myself though. This was only a wild guess and I felt guilty even thinking Alf was involved in a murder.

I walked towards the rubbish, my eyes searching the rubble.

There were torn black bags and bits of clothing and car tyres all stacked up. I looked to the very top of the pile, where decaying milk cartons and plastic bottles poked out.

'Jacki, what are you doing?' said Mum. 'Is that smell not killing you?'

That's when I saw them. Two of them. I couldn't believe it. But I couldn't investigate now. Mum would wonder what I was doing clawing through the rubbish. I would have to come back later.

The glorious weather continued on into the evening. Mum invited Des over to have dinner with us. I heard her on the phone and knew who she was talking to from her giddy voice. I'd been planning to go over to Colin's that evening so wasn't very happy when Mum told me I'd to eat with them. I tried to get out of it, but she insisted I stay there and make an effort to talk to Des. I texted Colin and then lay in a slump on the bed, waiting for the text to deliver.

'Jacki, will you stop moping around and go down to the shop for me?' said Mum. 'We're out of teabags.'

'All right,' I muttered, reaching for my bag, but then stopped abruptly. I couldn't risk seeing Nick. He probably thought I was completely insane and I wasn't sure how he might react. I would have to get Colin to scope it out before I went anywhere near him. There was no point in trying to explain everything to Nick, because my honest explanation was so weird.

'I can't go down there,' I said, flopping back on the bed. I knew it would make her mad, but that was the least of my worries.

'Why not?' said Mum, turning round.

'I don't want to talk about it.' I avoided her gaze.

'Fine. You'll have to watch the dinner then. And don't ask me for any favours this week.' She grabbed her purse from the table.

'But –'

'End of discussion.' Mum stormed out and I was left to watch the pasta and prepare the salad. Keeping all these secrets was proving hard work. There was no point in me telling her about Nick though, now that there was nothing to tell.

Des arrived early so I was forced to talk to him. At first it was tedious, but then I decided to be extra nice to him, in the hope of getting back on Mum's good side. She'd promised to take me shopping that weekend and I didn't want to mess it up. Once Mum saw that Des and I were getting on she might forget all about our little disagreement.

Des was all right, I suppose. He liked good music like Springsteen and Neil Young, his favourite film was *The Great Escape* and he used to play guitar when he was younger. He didn't play any more, but he had won an air guitar championship in Galway last year, which I had to admit was kind of cool. Apart from talking about movies and music, we talked about his mum. The fact that he was forty-eight and still living at home puzzled me, but I didn't pry. Des was besotted with my mum and she seemed to like him a lot. I was still not happy about them being together, but at least after getting to know him a little better the sight of the two of them didn't make me want to gag.

The evening went well, and thankfully Mum didn't seem mad at me any more. I offered to do the dishes, just to be extra sure. We went to bed soon after Des left, but Mum was in such a good mood she kept chatting to me. I was a bit distracted by what I was planning to do, but I had to wait until Mum was asleep.

Eventually she dozed off and I took the torch out of the cupboard and put on my grey sweater and Mum's wellies. I quietly stepped outside and closed the door behind me. I walked carefully along the dim path of torchlight, around the side of the house to the back garden. I was still amazed at how eerily still it was here at night. In our old house we lived on a quiet road, but you would still hear cars and people in the distance. Now you could go hours without hearing anything. I weaved through an obstacle course of building materials, then I looked up at the top of the big pile of rubbish. Sure enough, there they were: two leather bag handles poking out of the rubbish.

'*Fine . . . I'll burn the bloody bag. Whose is it anyway?*'

The colour was exactly the same as the chocolate-brown bag from my dream. I couldn't believe it. I had to have a closer look at them. I started to climb the pile, my fingernails desperately scraping at the dirt as I tried to hoist myself up. Bits of rubber and shards of plastic fell down on to the ground. I was trying not to tear any of the bin bags because they smelled disgusting. The smell was less potent without the sun on it, but it was still nauseating. I had no choice though. I had to grab hold of those two brown handles. Holding my breath, I lunged up and almost grasped them but then I lost my footing and fell to the ground.

'Ow!' I shouted as my shoulder hit the earth hard, but I was determined to try again. I scrambled back up the pile, quickly grabbed the handles and pulled them. A brown leather bag came free. Adrenalin pulsed through me at the sight of it. It was the same bag I'd seen in my nightmare.

I climbed back down and opened it. Then I let out a little shriek. Something had just scurried across my hand. A mouse. A tiny field mouse. I snapped the bag closed and hurried back towards the caravan, examining my new find on the way. There was a tear in the side, but other than that the bag seemed to be in pretty good condition. It was filthy and smelly though, so I couldn't take it into the caravan. I decided to stash it in the hedge, as Mum probably wouldn't come across it there. But first I sat down on the grass and opened it up.

Inside were four things: a black wallet, a packet of violin strings, a lipstick and a blue woolly hat. I took the lid off the lipstick. It was a bright red colour, half used. The hat was frayed at the bottom. The packet of violin strings was unopened and the price sticker was still on it – £12.50. I unzipped the wallet. There was just one thing in it – a small piece of paper that looked like it might have been a receipt, but the writing on it was too faded to make out. There were no cards, no photographs, no money. This was disappointing, but even without proof I knew who the bag belonged to. I could hardly believe it. I could hardly believe what I'd found.

> *Miss Jane had a bag*
> *And a mouse was in it.*
> *She opened the bag;*
> *He was out in a minute.*

Chapter 14

You notice different things when you get up early. I noticed how Des Butler locked his front door from the outside and double-checked that his sitting-room window was shut before getting into his van. I noticed that Mary Reynolds arrived at her shop at eight o'clock, even though she didn't open its doors until nine, and I noticed that Patrick Smyth kissed Brigid on the cheek, at the door of the guesthouse, before getting into his car and driving to work. From my position on the bench in the communal garden I could easily view the morning activities on the main street. I enjoyed observing the world, just watching what everybody was doing, without being part of it. It felt nice to be on the outskirts, to be invisible. I wondered if spirits liked doing that. Being able to go through the world unwatched, nobody knowing they were there. Well, apart from a few. People like Ger. People like me.

I loved the garden. I'd decided it was probably one of my favourite spots in Avarna. I felt a sense of security here that I didn't get anywhere else. And in the early mornings it seemed there was never anybody there. I could happily stay for ages. Relaxing. Watching.

The river glittered in the sunlight. It was beautiful from a distance but when I walked over and looked more closely I could see that the riverbed was a chaotic mixture of rock and stone, in grimy shades of brown, the outer beauty hiding a dark imperfect base. I picked up a flat stone and skimmed it into the water. It bounced along, sending soft waves rippling across the surface. I repeated this over and over again, then bent down and slid the tips of my fingers through the water. The riverbed seemed closer than it actually was. Just like Jane. Yesterday I had grown so sure that I could help her, but the more I thought about it the more I realized how little I knew. All morning I had been re-analyzing my dreams, reliving the attack and trying to identify any other signs she might have given me. The clues swirled around in my head, occasionally slotting together, but still not making an awful lot of sense.

Then I had an idea. I would write down what I knew so far. I took out my hardback notebook and flicked through the pages of lyrics until I found a blank space. I jotted down the few clues I had.

JANE
Attacked?
Murdered?
Connection with Beth? Murdered by the same person?
Leather bag
Bag contained: violin strings, purse, red lipstick and hat.
Sighted in: the forest
The Cupcake Café

When I wrote the clues down it didn't look as if there were very many at all. Ger said that there might be a link between the places that Jane appeared, but I couldn't think of any link between the dark forest and the cute Cupcake Café. I didn't like how there was no single way to solve this. I was used to problems that had a clear formula, a right and wrong answer. I could work out most maths problems in seconds, but I couldn't even seem to get started on this one. I had the bag, but it hadn't really offered me any new information. I was pretty sure the bag was vintage, so that would suggest that Jane was murdered some time ago. But I couldn't be certain. I don't know why but I also thought that the same person who killed Beth might have killed Jane too. But I knew from my Internet research, and from talking to Colin, that nobody seemed to know who had killed Beth. Maybe her killer was still in Avarna. Still walking around. That thought scared me a little, but it also gave me hope. If the killer was still here, then I had a better chance of finding them. I wondered what Jane had been like. What she'd looked like, what she'd liked to do. I wondered if she'd ever been in this garden, ever sat on this bench.

The gate creaked, bringing my thoughts back to the present. Colin came into the garden, carrying a bin bag and a rubbish picker. He didn't notice me sitting there. I watched as he picked up cigarette butts from the water's edge.

'Hi,' I said.

He looked over, surprised to see me. 'What are you doing up so early?' he asked, coming over and sitting beside me on the bench.

'Nothing really.' I closed my notebook and dropped it into my lap. 'What are you doing?'

'I told Mary I'd pick up any rubbish lying around here. She wants it looking spotless for the fête on Sunday. Nick was meant to do it for her, but he's at home sick. She was already stressing about the broken freezer in her shop so I decided to help her out.'

'What's wrong with Nick?' It hurt to say his name, but I wanted to make sure he was OK.

'Well, supposedly he has a migraine, but I bet he just fancied a lie-in. He was well able to go to the gig in Sligo with us last night. You should have come – it was deadly.'

'I had something on . . . So you're talking to Nick then? I was worried that maybe I'd caused trouble between you two.' I hoped that what had happened didn't come between them.

'I'm talking to him, but he's still pretty mad at me for almost breaking his nose with the door. He'll get over it.'

'Did he say anything about me?' I was aware I sounded kind of desperate, but I wanted to know.

'Em . . . no, not really.' Colin looked down at his shoes. He was a terrible liar.

'So he hates me?'

'Maybe just give him some space for a while. I know he didn't do anything to hurt you, but . . . what got into you anyway?'

'I just . . . I don't really want to talk about it.'

'Ooh, your songs!' said Colin, seeing 'Jacki's Lyrics' printed on the front of my notebook. He picked it up. 'Can I read them?' he asked, having already opened it. To my horror he was looking at my most recent entry.

'No, give it back.' I couldn't let him see it.

I went to grab the notebook, but Colin stood up and stepped backwards, pulling it out of my reach.

'Colin, please just give it back to me.'

'What is this?'

'Nothing just –'

He scanned down the page, his eyes widening. I tried to wrestle it from him, but it was already too late.

'Jacki, what's going on? Why do your lyrics look like a detective's notes?'

'I can't tell you. Just please give it back.'

'Why can't you tell me?' said Colin. 'We're mates.'

He held the notebook far above my head. I could tell he wasn't going to give up. This was it. He was going to think I had completely cracked. I took a deep breath.

'Prepare to think I am absolutely insane,' I said. 'Basically . . . I was getting these really bad headaches, so I went to the doctor –'

'Yeah, and I – your friend – went with you, remember?'

'Course, sorry . . .'

'And she said you had allergies.'

'Well, actually . . . I didn't really tell you the full story. She told me I might be dealing with something . . . something supernatural . . .'

'What?' He looked puzzled, his expression flickering between a smile and confusion.

'. . . and she sent me to Ger Rapple, the healer. Do you know him?'

'Yeah, well, I've heard of him. People come from all over the country to see him. He's supposed to be very good. What did she mean by "something supernatural"?'

'Well . . . I'm getting to that. At first I didn't want to go and see Ger, because I didn't believe in any of that stuff. But then something really weird happened to me in the bedroom at David's. I felt like I was being attacked, and my body was on the bed, but my mind was somewhere else – like in the forest.

After that I got really scared, so I went to see Ger and he told me that a girl called Jane is trying to contact me. She was murdered and her spirit needs my help to move on. I think she wants me to find out who murdered her, so that she can finally be at peace.' I just blurted it out, aware of how it all sounded. 'I know you believe in ghosts, but I don't expect you to believe this. It's crazy, but I swear it's true.'

Colin read the page again. It felt like an eternity until he finally spoke.

'I do believe it,' he said.

'Really?' This totally took me by surprise.

'Yes. I know you well enough by now, Jacki. If you say this is happening, then I believe you.'

'Thanks. That means a lot.'

'I'll try to help you any way I can.'

I was almost crying with relief. Colin could sense this, so he tried to lighten the mood a bit.

'I can be your sidekick!' he exclaimed. 'I'm cute, I'm funny . . . I'd be perfect for it! What do you think?'

'I'm just glad you don't think I'm mental,' I said with a sniff. 'But don't tell anyone else, OK? Can we just keep this between us?'

'I won't tell anybody. I promise.'

'Thanks,' I said, wiping my eyes.

We sat in silence for a few moments. I had to stop crying in front of people. It was becoming too much of a habit.

'Anyway . . . on a lighter note,' said Colin. 'Emily is having some people over to her house this evening. She lives a good bit outside the village, so I'll get Mam to drop us if you want to come.'

'Sorry, Colin . . . I can't.'

'Don't be silly. You're coming to Emily's.'

'No, I'm not. I can't face Nick. Not yet. See, he isn't just some guy . . . I'm crazy about him. I can't stop thinking about him. It really hurts.' I hated the thought of having to sit across from Nick while he ignored me or, even worse, tried to force an explanation out of me.

'I didn't realize you liked him that much,' said Colin. 'But don't worry – he won't be there. It's a girls' night in.'

'But you're going?'

'Obviously,' said Colin with a smile. 'And so are you, even if I have to kidnap you and drag you there myself.'

'I'm really sorry . . . but I don't feel like going anywhere.'

'But Emily's dad is an expert on local history. He wrote a book about Avarna a few years ago. Maybe he'll have some info on Jane. I'm sure he'll be there tonight.'

I thought about it for a moment. To my surprise, my sense of duty to Jane was just enough to sway me.

'Fine, I'll go then,' I said. 'But only for a little while.'

I was actually a little excited that Emily's dad was a historian. If there was someone called Jane from Avarna who had been murdered, then he'd surely know about it.

I went to meet Mum for lunch in the Cupcake Café. I was early so I thought I'd use a computer for a while. Mary was sitting at one of the tables with her eight-year-old daughter, Rosie, who I'd heard all about on one of my visits to the shop. I smiled at them as I walked towards the bathroom. I wanted to see if Jane would come back.

I stood behind the door, whispering her name over and over.

140

Deep down I knew she wasn't coming back. Not yet anyway. The eerie sensation of the other day just wasn't there any more. I hated the thought of her being stuck in that in-between stage, slipping back and forth between this world and whatever was waiting for her in the next. I wanted her to come back. I wanted to tell her that I was going to find out who'd murdered her, no matter how long it took. I tried to imagine her, tried to remember even the slightest detail from our encounter. She had black hair – that's all I knew.

I eventually gave up, but there was still no sign of Mum so I logged on to a computer. I searched *jane murdered avarna* and all its variations but found nothing. I wasn't too disappointed though. I was hopeful that Emily's dad would be able to give me some information, or at least point me in the right direction.

So I just messed around for a bit. Emily had uploaded pictures from the gig in Sligo the night before. I clicked through the photos, smiling at the ones of Emily and the lads pulling stupid faces. But I didn't smile at the next one. I recognized his red hoodie immediately. There he was . . . eating the face off some blonde girl. She was wearing a slutty belly-top and his hands were all over her.

I felt sick . . . so confused, jealous, angry. I logged off and just needed to get out of there.

'Ali, if you see my mum would you mind telling her that I had to leave early? Thanks,' I said, before hurrying out of the café, slamming the door behind me. I was definitely forgetting about him now.

As I hurried home, I felt angry and upset, but at the same time I felt a strange sense of relief. Nick had found someone else. I could forget about him now. I could stop thinking about him all the time. I could stop obsessing about how I was going to explain myself to him. This was exactly what I needed. I didn't need anything distracting me from my duty to Jane. Being crazy about someone was a distraction. A horrible, unhealthy distraction. I was done with boys. It always, always ended badly. I didn't need them in my life. Or else, I'd keep them there, but never get attached. I'd be like Hannah: always the dumper, never the dumpee. Always the one to turn them down, never the one sitting staring at the phone, waiting for them to text. I'd be the one who'd forget to text *them* back. I'd be the one who forgot their birthdays, forgot their numbers, forgot their names even. I picked a yellow flower from the ditch and ripped off the petals one by one. *I don't love him. I don't love him. I don't love him.* Unfortunately, with every petal plucked, my initial rage started to dwindle. And it was just replaced with hurt. But the thought of Nick with that girl was enough to at least dull my obsession. Although I knew I wasn't going to be able to forget about him, I was at least going to try.

Chapter 15

I spent that evening in the caravan making flyers. I wanted Mum to think I was at least interested in finding something to do for the summer. Besides, I could really have done with the extra cash. Freelance ghost whispering wasn't proving the most lucrative occupation. And I needed to keep my mind as far away as possible from you know who. I finally finished the flyers, managing to get glitter-glue everywhere in the process.

Singer Available for All Occasions
Weddings, Parties, Funerals etc.
Unique Style and Diverse Repertoire
Contact Jacki King on 080 324519

My phone buzzed. It was such a rare occurrence in the caravan that it made me jump. The one bar of coverage that came and went must have decided to come back. It was a message from Emily, asking if I wanted to sleep at her house tonight, as a few of the girls from St Mary's were staying over. Maybe I could talk to her about that photo of Nick. But I decided that dwelling on it would do no good whatsoever. Plus she would want to know the whole story about what had happened in the bedroom, and I couldn't tell her that. I was excited about getting to know my new schoolmates, but wondered if Mum would let me sleep there. Ever since I'd disguised staying at Cian's as an all-night birthday celebration at Hannah's, Mum had been extremely wary of sleepovers.

'Mum, can I stay over at Emily's? It's just the girls staying over. And her parents will be there and –'

'No problem,' said Mum. 'You enjoy yourself.'

What? No request for Emily's exact address? No demand to ring her parents to check everything was above board? Maybe now that I was nearly sixteen she had more faith in me.

I heard a car drive in and looked out the window. It wasn't a car. It was a van. A familiar van. Now I knew why Mum was so happy to be rid of me for the night. Ew.

'I'm not a taxi service,' said Brigid, picking up the stick of glue and pasting another photograph on to the giant collage. Lydia flicked through one of the photo albums from the stack on the table, choosing the occasional picture that was worthy of inclusion in the collage to be displayed at Mary's fiftieth birthday party. She was wearing an awesome pink mini-dress and bright red boots. Those colours really shouldn't have worked together, but they did on Lydia.

'Emily's house is so far away,' said Colin. 'And it's lashing rain.'

'It's drizzling,' said Brigid. 'Why do you always have to be so dramatic?'

'I am not!' said Colin, throwing his arms up in exasperation.

'Look at this one!' said Lydia, holding up a photograph of a couple kissing. The girl was wearing a yellow jacket with extreme shoulder pads and the guy was sporting some really severe sideburns.

'Who's that with Mary?' asked Colin.

'That's Joe Clancy.'

'No way!' I said.

'They used to go out,' said Brigid. 'Joe and Michael even had a fight over her out in the main street once. The entire village saw it.'

'Maybe I should leave this one where it is,' said Lydia, slotting the photograph back into the album.

Mary had been a pretty young woman, with rosy cheeks and long curly brown hair. If you ignored the dodgy fashion, she looked lovely in all the pictures.

'Our mother always had a camera out,' said Brigid. 'There are probably more pictures of Mary here than in her own house.'

'Right, enough with the trip down memory lane,' said Colin. 'We're late.'

Brigid and Lydia pointed to the half-empty bottle of wine on the table. 'We couldn't drop you even if we wanted to,' said Brigid.

Colin rolled his eyes and took out his phone.

'I'll see how Carla's getting there,' he said as he began scrolling through his phonebook. I didn't know David's sister was a friend of Emily's – she seemed much younger. I really hoped Amanda wasn't going too. She was so irritating.

'Hey,' said Colin, 'any chance we could get a lift to Emily's with you? OK, cool. Thanks! Bye!' He hung up. 'Her dad's taking us,' said Colin. 'They'll be here in ten minutes.'

*

Peter Mulvey was pretty much what I expected from a high-flying business executive. He drove a flashy car, wore an expensive suit and kept his designer sunglasses on even at dusk. I sat in the passenger seat in silence while Carla and Colin chatted loudly in the back. It turned out Carla was on Emily's hockey team, and thankfully hadn't brought Amanda along.

'Mary was telling me that your back garden is in a bit of a state?' said Peter, eventually making conversation. 'I know a very good waste-removal company that could help you with that.'

'I think my mum's got it sorted, thanks,' I said. Despite my best efforts I couldn't stop thinking about Nick. The thought of him with that girl made me sick. At least there was no chance of me having to see him tonight.

'Find anything interesting?' said Peter.

'Sorry?'

'In your garden. Mary was saying there were all sorts of things buried under there. Did you find anything interesting?'

'No,' I said, perhaps a little too abruptly. 'Nothing at all. You don't want to get too close to it anyway – it really smells.' I felt dizzy again and my headache was coming back. I tried my best to ignore it, looking out the window as we sped past the fields.

Peter pulled up right to the door. I could see into the sitting room – there were lots of girls already there. Colin and I thanked Peter for the lift, then I grabbed my rucksack and stepped out into the rain.

'Well now, let me see . . .' said Emily's dad, Henry. He was a small man with a balding head and huge glasses. 'There have been five murders recorded in these parts since 1960. Kathleen Brogan, suffocated by her husband, Charles. Mary Hughes, hit over the head by a burglar, died instantly. Francis Quinn, shot in the back of the head while out hunting, and Poppy Gilleece, stabbed by her half-sister in a jealous rage. I explore all these murders in more detail in my book. There has been only one unsolved case – the murder of Beth Cullen.' My heart sank as he continued. 'I'm afraid, Colin, that an investigative project entitled *Unsolved Murders in Avarna* would leave you examining only one incident. Five is actually quite a high number of murders for a village area. There must be something in the water,' he joked.

Emily dropped the remainder of a packet of marshmallows into a giant bowl and started to pour out ten mugs of hot chocolate. 'Let's hope not,' she said.

'I'll have to advise you to pick another topic for your school history project,' added Henry.

Colin nodded. 'I think you're right, thanks.'

'Why are you talking about school?' asked Emily.

'I like to get started during the summer,' said Colin. 'I just can't get enough of schoolwork!' He sounded so convincing I almost believed him.

'Hear that, Emily?' said Henry. 'Maybe you should put down those novels of yours and start doing your history project!'

'Colin, I didn't know you chose hist–'

'I'll help you with those,' said Colin, taking the tray of mugs and signalling for her to keep quiet.

'You are so strange,' she muttered.

Emily's friends were all very nice. I tried to memorize their names and join in the chatter, only occasionally letting my mind wander back to Nick. I wondered what he was doing tonight.

Probably trying to figure out how he'd ever fancied such a complete nutter. He could think whatever he liked now though, I didn't care. Well, I tried to convince myself that I didn't.

By the end of the night I was no closer to finding out who Jane was, but, on the upside, I had got to know Emily's friends. We stayed up until four o'clock, watching *Gossip Girl* reruns and eating chocolate ice cream. One of Emily's best friends played drums, and she was thinking of getting a band together. School was just a few weeks away, but now it didn't seem like such a major deal. The girls had advised me who to befriend and who to avoid, and told me which teachers were all right and which ones to watch out for. I wished that school was the only thing I had to worry about.

I had thought that perhaps sleeping in a different house would mean I'd be spared the nightmare. On the contrary, it had been exactly the same. The next morning, just like every morning, I woke up feeling as if I'd been in a fistfight, my head thumping and my body aching. I'd dreamed of the body pushing down on me, shoving my head into the cold ground, and bits of bark digging into my bare legs.

Back in the caravan, I caught a glimpse of my reflection in the bathroom mirror and winced. I looked pale, not a stunning pale like Lydia, but a sickly pale. My face was drained. I picked up Mum's blusher and dusted it on to my cheeks, giving them an artificial rosy glow. My eyeliner helped distract from the tired look in my eyes. There was one positive sign – the bruises had faded. They were hardly even visible now. They had served their purpose: Jane had got my attention. I had time to spare, time which I didn't want to spend focusing on my mounting problems. I took out my guitar and began strumming and singing softly, each word of my song slowly pushing all the other stuff out of my head.

> *'Confusion is a lonely place;*
> *I'm looking but can't see her face.*
> *She pulled me in and kept me close;*
> *Her beauty is a troubled ghost.*
> *All I saw was her and me;*
> *We kept each other company,*
> *Looking for the right way out.*
> *She whispers but I wish she'd shout.'*

My phone buzzed in my pocket and I looked at the message. It was from Colin, and simply said JANE UPDATE. I texted back TELL ME! and waited a few moments for his reply. MY HOUSE. NOW.

I left the caravan so fast I didn't even remember to take my iPod, and I always took that everywhere. I desperately wanted to find out what Colin knew. When I got to the guesthouse he was alone in the kitchen making coffee.

'Hey,' he said. 'You're not going to believe this.' He pointed to a note on the table in front of me.

The paper was pale pink. Probably from a cute little letter set, one that made you want to get a pen pal just so you could have an excuse to buy it. Little pink hearts formed a border round the page, although their colour had faded with time. The handwriting was small and neat.

I picked up the note and read it aloud.

Dear Audrey,
Please forgive me. I am so sorry.
Please talk to me.
Love always,
Jane x

My eyes fixed on the final word.

'Where did you get this?' I asked, my heart thumping.

'In the attic. Mam asked me to go up and look for more photographs, and I found this in among a pile of Lydia's stuff.

'Who's Audrey?'

'No idea. My mam said she doesn't know anyone called Audrey. My dad didn't have a clue either.'

'Did you ask Lydia?'

'Not yet, but we could ask her now,' said Colin as we spotted Lydia heading for the dining room. She jumped when she saw us sitting in the semi-darkness. She was carrying a red silk dress, its plunging neckline sparkling with diamanté studs.

'Lydia, have you ever seen this before?' Colin asked, holding up the notepaper. She came over to the table and peered at it. Her face seemed to get paler. She scanned down through the words. There was some recognition there – I was sure of it.

'No, never seen it before,' she shrugged. Her hands gripped the dress more tightly.

'I found it in your box in the attic,' said Colin. I kept staring at Lydia. She definitely seemed a little bit flustered.

'Do you know who Audrey is?' I asked.

'Nope.'

'What about Jane? Did you know anybody called Jane?'

'No offence, guys,' she said with a smile, 'but I really don't have time to chat about a letter you two found in the attic. I have to finish this dress I'm making Mary for her birthday.' Lydia walked out the door.

'She knows something,' I whispered.

'Definitely,' said Colin, folding up the note and dropping it into my pocket.

Chapter 16

Mum and I had gone for dinner to Clancy's pub. She was tired and we both needed a break from our cramped living quarters. It was nearly ten o'clock, and Mum was enjoying an after-dinner drink. It was relatively quiet; there were two couples I didn't know finishing off a late meal, and Mary and Lydia were sitting at the table behind me. They were the most unlikely best friends in the world. Mary was so prim and organized; Lydia so cool and carefree. Lydia had said hi to us when she came in, but wasn't her usual friendly self. I was sure she knew something about that note. I was close enough to overhear what they were saying, but couldn't really concentrate when Mum was chatting to me. When two of Mum's new teacher friends came in and joined us I had a chance to eavesdrop on Lydia and Mary's conversation.

'Do you have any cocktails, Joe?' asked Mary, her elbows resting on the table.

'Where do you think you are?' Joe joked with them.

Mary sighed. 'Fine! We'll have two more white wines, please.'

'Coming right up,' said Joe, and then disappeared through the door behind the bar.

'And remember that time,' said Mary, 'the three of us snuck

off to the disco in Drumshanbo, and we would have got away with it if Beth hadn't forgotten her bloody key!'

I couldn't believe my luck. They were actually talking about Beth. Maybe I'd learn something more about her. Even if she wasn't the spirit who needed my help. I was intrigued.

'Oh, that was hilarious!' said Lydia. 'I got in so much trouble over that. But it was worth it. One of the best nights ever. We should go out more, you know. We used to go out all the time.'

'I wish I could,' mumbled Mary. 'But it's nice that we go out for Beth's birthday, no matter what.'

'To Beth,' said Mary.

'To Beth!' said Lydia, and they clinked glasses.

'Lydia,' Mary paused. 'Do you think she's . . . you know . . . looking down on us?'

'I like to think she is. I'll never forget it, Mary. The day she went missing. I'll never forget it as long as I live. I wish I hadn't fought with her . . . that I'd just gone shopping like she'd asked.'

'You can't keep blaming yourself,' said Mary. 'It wasn't your fault. You weren't to know something terrible was going to happen.'

Lydia took another sip of her drink. 'Do you have any idea who did it?'

'No,' whispered Mary. 'I don't.'

'There you go,' said Joe, placing two tall glasses on the table.

'What's this?' asked Lydia.

'You made us cocktails!' said Mary.

'I tried my best. May not be what you're used to, but –'

'Thank you!' said Lydia.

'What's it called?' asked Mary. 'What kind is it?'

'A bloody Mary! What else?'

Mary found this hilarious and started laughing hysterically.

Lydia took a sip from her blood-red drink.

'Go on, Mary, have a sip.'

Mary took a gulp from her glass, then twirled the little party umbrella sticking out from it.

'You're brilliant, Joe,' she said.

'Ah, would you stop,' he chuckled as he went back out through the door.

'Imagine,' said Lydia, turning to Mary. 'Yourself and Joe could have been an item.'

'Yes, I know,' she sighed. 'You never know what turns your life will take, do you?'

There was a loud burst of laughter that drowned out the conversation. Suddenly I realized I was sitting at a table of teachers. I could tell they were censoring their gossip for my benefit, so I decided to go out for some air and leave them to it.

Joe was standing outside, smoking a cigarette.

'Jacki!' he said. 'I have something to ask you. We saw your poster in the parish hall, and myself and Brigid would love to hire you for the party, just to sing one song. We already have the band, but I think Mary would love it if you sang too.'

Oh no. I had planned to avoid the party. I didn't want to hang out around Nick any time soon. But Joe looked so enthusiastic that I found myself saying, 'I'd love to!'

'Great!' Joe took out a little crumpled piece of paper from his pocket. On it was a list of ten song titles written in red pen.

'These are a few she likes.'

'How did you get the list?'

'I made it myself. I know all of Mary's favourites. Just pick whichever one you like.'

'OK, thanks. How're the party preparations going?' I asked as I put it in my pocket.

'They're going great. We still have a lot to do though.'

'And Mary still has no idea about the party?'

'Not a clue. She wanted to organize a Tidy Village Committee meeting for Friday, but everybody kept saying they had other stuff on. She was in a right huff yesterday! I can't wait to see the look on her face. It's going to be priceless.'

'How are you going to get her there so?' I asked.

Joe checked over his shoulder to make sure Mary was with Lydia at the bar and well out of earshot. 'Well, you know her husband, Michael, the sergeant – he's going to pretend to be taking her out to dinner, and then he'll say that he has to drop something off in the hall, and then he'll come out to Mary and say that I want to talk to her for a minute, and we'll all be there when she comes in!'

'She'll be delighted.'

'I hope so,' said Joe, flicking his cigarette ash on to the ground.

'Joe . . . do you know anything about the Beth Cullen murder?'

He looked at me strangely. 'That's a bit out of the blue! Why do you ask?'

'I overheard Lydia and Mary talking about it just now, and I've seen her name mentioned in a couple of places.'

Joe sighed. 'That was a long time ago . . . yet in ways it's like yesterday. Do you not know what happened to her?'

'I know she was murdered and her body was found in the forest.'

'Yes, and she was . . . well, you know . . .'

'She was what?'

'She was . . . she was molested,' whispered Joe, his voice quivering on the last word. 'From the . . . *evidence* left on her body they were able to determine the blood type of the killer . . . they took blood samples from all the men around here to try and find a match. I gave a sample, along with all the other men in the village.'

'But they didn't find a match?'

'Well, I suppose they narrowed it down to a certain number, but they didn't have enough evidence to charge anybody.'

'Why didn't they do DNA testing?'

'That wasn't available back then.' Joe took a puff from his cigarette. 'Personally I didn't think anyone from around here would be capable of murder . . . But the human mind is a strange thing . . . You never know what will make somebody snap.'

Chapter 17

I was resting on one of our patio recliners practising Van Morrison's 'Have I Told You Lately' for Mary's party. I sat cross-legged, playing my guitar. I loved my guitar – it sounded awesome and was pretty much an extension of me. I played it so much that it looked kind of battered. My gran had bought me a guitar case for my birthday. Reluctantly, because she'd wanted me to learn piano. I'd gone for a few lessons, and knew the basics, but guitar was my first love. As I practised the song over and over, I wondered why Mary and Joe hadn't ended up together. I was sure they would have made a sweet couple. I'd seen Sergeant Reynolds around the village, and had to admit he was more handsome, but Joe Clancy was so nice.

'Jacki,' said Mum. 'I like that song, but if I hear it one more time I will have to bash you over the head with that guitar. Could you not play something different?'

'Oh, I forgot to tell you,' I said. 'I have my first paid gig. I'm singing at Mary's fiftieth. Remember you told me to be enterprising?'

'That's great! Congratulations! But you had that song

perfect half an hour ago. Play me one of your own. I haven't heard a new one in ages.' Mum sat up and adjusted her sunglasses.

'OK,' I said, tuning my guitar. 'By the way . . . I need new strings.'

'So your first gig is costing me money?' said Mum with a sigh.

'I'll pay you back.'

'Go on then, let's hear it.'

What had started as an upbeat love song had now morphed into a bleak ballad, but I sang it nonetheless.

> *'This tough love is making me*
> *Give up, it's breaking me*
> *Deep in the shadows I hide.*
>
> *Love is a losing game,*
> *Dirty cold ruleless game,*
> *Lost in one blink of an eye.*
>
> *"I love you" he said but my*
> *Heart it still bled; this was*
> *Pain I couldn't ignore.*
>
> *So no tears left my eyes when*
> *I lay by his side and said,*
> *"Baby, I love you no more."'*

'Very nice, Jacki, good lyrics.'

'Thanks, Mum!'

'I almost forgot, can you go down to the shop to get stamps and post these letters for me?' She rooted around in her handbag and pulled out two envelopes.

'That's it? That's all you have to say about my song?'

'You know I think all your songs are great. But I really have to get these in the post.'

'Sorry, Mum, I can't go down to the shop.' I pulled the guitar strap off over my head and put the guitar back in its case.

'Why, what's up? Is something wrong?'

I wanted to tell her, but if I told her one thing I'd have to tell her everything. So I decided against it.

'Long story,' I said, zipping up the case.

'Well, you can either go down to the shop or there's a pile of dishes mounting up inside.' I looked up at Mum, hoping she was joking, but her stare confirmed that she wasn't.

'Fine! I'll go then.'

When I got to the door of the shop I took a deep breath, pushed it open and stepped inside. There was nobody there.

I heard some activity and voices out the back.

'For God's sake, Mary!' a man's voice bellowed from inside the storeroom. They mustn't have heard me come in. My heart pounded. I stood still, behind one of the shelves, unsure of what to do next.

'Michael, please . . . please just calm down,' said Mary.

It was her husband who was yelling at her. Part of me wanted to quickly leave . . . to get as far away as possible, but another part of me needed to stay and listen.

'How dare you . . . how dare you bring that murderer on to my premises?'

Murderer? Had I heard that right? Michael's voice frightened me. It had a quality that made me shiver.

'I didn't ask him to come in. He just happened to be in the shop the morning it broke. Who told you that –'

'Oh, so you didn't think I'd find out?'

'No . . . I . . .' Mary's voice was shaking. 'He offered to help. I could hardly say no. He was only here for a few minutes . . . He fixed it in no time . . . I couldn't afford to wait.' Mary paused and then continued with slightly more force in her voice. 'Besides there was never any proof that he –'

I heard a dull thud, something being thrown on the floor. Then I thought I heard a whimpering sound.

'You know as well as I do . . .' Michael was yelling, 'he didn't have an alibi for that night. Half the village knows he did it. That should be enough for you . . . What is it going to look like . . . you hiring him to fix our bloody freezer? A killer on my premises. You're so stupid sometimes.'

There was silence.

'You didn't have one either,' she said.

'Excuse me?'

'You didn't have an alibi for that night either, Michael.'

There was another loud crash and Mary yelped.

'How dare you,' said Michael. 'Keep your mouth shut. And if you ever invite Des Butler into this shop again, you will be very, very sorry.'

The storeroom door swung open and Sergeant Reynolds stormed out of the shop, completely ignoring me.

Moments later Mary emerged from the storeroom with her signature cheerful smile plastered across her face.

*

I needed to talk to someone about this. Fast. I bought the stamps and left in a hurry. I knocked on the door of the guesthouse but nobody answered. So I tried Lydia's shop. I could hear The Cure blasting out from the speakers before I even opened the door. The workshop curtain was pulled back, and Lydia was at the sewing machine. She looked up, and must have seen the worried look on my face, because she turned off the stereo straight away.

'Jacki, are you OK?'

'No, I'm not really,' I said. 'I just heard something really upsetting.'

'What's wrong?' said Lydia, hurrying over and putting her arm round my shoulders. I felt like I was going to faint. I couldn't believe what I had just heard. It took me a few seconds before I could get the words out.

'Did Des Butler kill somebody?' Saying it out loud made me feel even worse. 'Who told you that?' Lydia sounded kind of angry.

'I overheard Sergeant Reynolds say something.'

'Some people think he did,' said Lydia. 'But not everyone thinks so.' She pulled out a stool from under her desk and offered it to me. I sat down, but still felt faint.

'Why do they think that? Who did he kill? He's working on my house. My mum has been on dates with him!' I couldn't understand why nobody had told us this.

'He was a main suspect for Beth's murder,' said Lydia. 'But no one in my family believes it. He would never have hurt Beth. Michael Reynolds's opinion is not everybody's opinion.'

'Beth Cullen . . .?' I couldn't believe that Des was a suspect.

'Yes.' Lydia sat down on her swivel chair, weaving a piece of blue fabric between her fingers.

'If he was a main suspect, then there must have been some reason –'

'The partner is often a main suspect.'

'Des and Beth were . . . together?' This was too much. I just couldn't believe it.

'They were childhood sweethearts.' Lydia smiled when she said this. I couldn't understand why she was so calm. Surely, in this instance, a police officer's opinion would be a good one to take? I didn't particularly like Sergeant Reynolds, but he must have had a reason for suspecting Des.

This was crazy. Des was going out with my mum. I was pretty sure she really liked him. I just couldn't understand why nobody had told us this sooner.

'If he didn't do it, then who did?' I asked.

'The killer hasn't been found,' said Lydia flatly. 'But I know Des isn't capable of murder. You and Rachel have nothing to worry about. He didn't do it.' She sounded so sure.

Nevertheless I couldn't just ignore what I'd heard. I would have to tell Mum. How on earth was I going to tell her that the guy she really likes and has been dating was a suspected murderer?

I made the walk back home last as long as I could. I wanted to let Mum have a few more carefree minutes. Also, I had to decide the best way to tell her. She might think I was overreacting, exaggerating whatever I'd heard because I didn't want her to go out with Des any more. She thought I didn't like him. But the truth was I'd got to like him a lot and thought he was a really nice guy. I didn't want Mum to go out with anyone, but I guess, if she was going to date, it might as well be someone like Des. That was before I'd gone into the shop of course.

Before I'd overheard Sergeant Reynolds. I put in my earphones and played some music to help me focus. To help me figure out what I was going to say.

When I got back to the caravan Mum was crouched down, rooting through the cupboard.

'I'm making pancakes,' she said. 'Want one?'

'No, thanks,' I answered. I took a deep breath.

'Is there something up?' she said, abandoning her search and standing up. She must have known there was something wrong as pancakes were a favourite of mine.

'There's something I have to tell you . . .' The details all came pouring out: what I'd overheard in the shop and what Lydia had said. Mum's eyes widened, and for a few seconds she said nothing. When she eventually spoke her reaction was pretty much the same as mine.

'Why did nobody tell us this?' she said, sitting down at the table and shaking her head in disbelief. She didn't sound as angry as me – just really upset.

'Not everybody thinks he did it,' I said. 'But Sergeant Reynolds seemed pretty sure he's guilty. I think you should be careful, Mum.'

'I will be,' she answered. She went back to making pancakes and didn't say anything else about it for the rest of the evening.

Chapter 18

Candy floss – possibly one of the greatest foods in the world. A delightfully fluffy little cloud of sugar. Sticky and sweet and wonderful. Colin and I walked around the fête with two huge helpings of it, struggling to protect it from the crowds of people milling down the main street. The road had been closed to cars for the day and stalls now spanned its length, selling everything from handmade jewellery to chocolate-chip muffins. At one table you could get a henna tattoo and at another you could learn how a bodhrán is made. You could get your fortune told or your tealeaves read; you could buy a friendship bracelet or a patchwork quilt, a crystal to hang in your window or a framed photograph to put on your wall. The fête didn't have one particular theme: it was a wonderful mish-mash of all kinds of different things.

Multicoloured bunting joined the buildings and helium heart and star-shaped balloons were tied to each stall, trying to break free into the overcast sky. Mary stood in the middle of the crowd, staring up at a grey cloud hovering overhead, with a look that said *Don't you dare try to ruin my fête*. She really had done a super job in organizing this event, but there was nothing she could do about the weather. She whipped a black walkie-talkie off her belt and spoke into it. 'Check the rain cover for the generator. Over.'

A stage had been erected in front of the hall. Music was to be played there all day and a list of acts and times was written on a chalkboard beside the steps. Upcoming performances ranged from a string quartet to a gospel choir to a group of guys doing Metallica covers. The headliners were the highly respected Avarna Céilí Band, and I was really looking forward to seeing them. Right now a swing band was treating the crowd to a rendition of 'I'm All Shook Up'. Huge speakers ensured they could be heard throughout the village.

To the left of the stage there was a mini fairground. Little kids lined up to go on the carousel, the swing boats moved to and fro to the beat of the music and little twinkling red lights illuminated the sign for the funhouse. There was a ghost train too, and as the train came out of the little tunnel I could see Emily and David sitting in it, squashed together and not looking frightened at all. And behind them were Nick and Simon, laughing loudly, hanging out of the side of the train. I still found myself as attracted to Nick as ever, even though I hated him for kissing that girl. I couldn't help still wanting him.

'Let's go back to the stalls,' I said, before Colin noticed them. I didn't really want to be near Nick, even if I did still have feelings for him. We headed back down the road, and Colin's eyes were drawn to the cake stand. We surveyed the éclairs and chocolate cakes and Colin decided to buy a caramel square.

'So much for my diet,' said Colin, mid chew.

'Would you shut up? You're so skinny,' I said.

'I'm two double cheeseburgers away from full-on love handles.'

I breathed in all the different smells – corn on the cob, crêpes, hotdogs, but didn't eat anything. My stomach was unsettled, just like it had been during those strange incidents in the forest and in the Cupcake Café. This time I wasn't frightened though. I felt strange, but weirdly calm at the same time. There was an edge to this sickening feeling that was almost addictive. I welcomed it. It meant she was back.

I looked for any signs, any clues that I could add to the collection I already had. Colin wanted to find Jane too, but he wasn't thinking about her now. He wanted to help her, but he could just as easily have forgotten about her. For me she was a continual concern.

People flocked to the centre of the village – locals and tourists, former residents and relatives of current ones. Sarah walked past us in a stunning pink dress, and didn't even look in our direction. I thought it was more out of embarrassment than bitchiness though. She had hardly spoken a word to anyone in the group since the break-up. She looked pretty miserable. I still reckoned she would win the Miss Avarna title. Her flawless skin, brown eyes and tiny frame meant she already looked like a celebrity. The judges would adore her.

'Let's check this out,' I said, pointing at the table with a banner that read GUESSING STALL. Rita Clancy was sitting behind the table, on which stood a glass jar full of marbles, a giant ball of wool and a porcelain doll.

'Are you going to have a go?' she asked me. 'You have to guess how many marbles there are –' she pointed to the jar – 'how long that is –' she pointed to the blue ball of wool – 'and what this little lady's name is.' She pointed to the porcelain doll. 'Write down your name and phone number too so I can phone

you if you win.' She handed me a pencil and a slip of paper. I
wrote down:

256
50 metres

I picked up the doll to have a closer look. It had curly black hair
and wore a frilly peach-coloured dress and a beige coat with
two gold buttons. She was a bit scary, with glassy green eyes
that looked straight at me.

I scribbled down the word Jane and gave my guesses to Rita.
She popped them in a cardboard box along with the other
entries.

The Miss Avarna contestants were huddled round the stage,
preparing to learn their fate in less than half an hour. They
wore huge smiles, some genuine, some blatantly fake.

'She cannot get away with that,' said Colin, pointing to a
girl in an unflatteringly clingy dress. 'And that does nothing for
her,' he added, pointing to an ill-fitting halter dress.

'Shhh!' I said. 'They'll hear you.'

I followed Colin under the balloon arch into the fairground.
We waved to Chris, who was working there for the day. He was
helping a little kid out of a bumper car and looked totally
bored.

'Let's queue for that,' Colin suggested, pointing to the carousel where there was still a long line of children waiting.

'What's over there?' I asked, having spotted the sign that read
FOTO FUN. Colin trailed after me as we pushed through the
crowd.

'It's a photo booth!' I said.

It had a red velvet curtain and for four euro it promised a variety of fun photo options. You could get a tropical paradise background, your head in an astronaut uniform, or feature in your very own movie poster.

'You can see what you'd look like as a Manga character!' said Colin, pulling back the curtain and sitting on the swivel seat with the cracked leather cover. He chose the Manga option and posed.

'Deadly!' he said, when the screen showed him with big eyes, a pointed chin and a thin nose. He put the money in and clicked print.

'You go,' he said.

My Manga character looked a lot like me, but with a triangular face, accentuated eyebrows and small blood-red lips.

'I should do a painting of these,' said Colin.

'Let's get one of the two of us together,' I said, rooting in my purse for change. The seat was barely big enough for one so I sat on Colin's knee.

'I'm not in it,' said Colin. 'Scooch down.'

'You are in it. I'm not – you move,' I said with a giggle.

'You totally have more screen space than me.'

'Right, smile!'

Colin playfully pushed me out of the booth and waited for the photos to come out. There we were, Colin and I, our faces squished together, me sporting the biggest smile ever, Colin sticking his tongue out. But there was something strange about it because hovering above our heads, just over us, was the outline of a blurred face. A blurred face with long black hair.

Colin nearly dropped the photo.

'What is that?' he said. 'What background did I press?'

'It's OK. It's her,' I said. She was back. She was definitely here.

Before Colin could react he heard someone call his name.

'Colin!' shouted Mary Reynolds. 'Just the person I was looking for.'

'Me?' Colin's voice was shaky.

'Yes, Bob was meant to be judging the art show, but he's sick. Would you mind filling in for him? It's just this way.'

Before Colin could protest, Mary was pulling him in the direction of the art tent, and I was left there, still looking at the photograph. I could tell that Colin was freaked out, but I wasn't scared. I just wanted to help her. As the ink dried, her face started to fade, and soon all that was left was a light grey mark above our heads, so light that you would hardly even notice it.

The second-hand bookstall had lots of good stuff. I got a copy of Slash's autobiography for only three euro and I bought a thriller for Mum. I was sorry she was missing the fête; it was a lot of fun. But she'd said she just wasn't in the mood for it and didn't want to risk running into Des after what I'd told her.

Mary Reynolds's voice echoed from the speakers. 'The Miss Avarna Presentation will take place in ten minutes.' There were a few excited gasps from the huddle of contestants. Colin was still in the art tent, so I went over to see how he was doing.

The children's art competition entries were tacked up on a white board that spanned the width of the tent. I scanned the assortment of juvenile doodles and paintings.

'Right,' said Colin. 'I have to pick a first, second and third. Oh, and two highly commended ones.' He showed me the little bunch of rosettes. I didn't envy his job. I'd never been very good at art. I could appreciate it, but I had no idea how to judge it. There were drawings of horses and sheep and houses and flowers and one that looked like it might be a spaceship.

The tent was eerily silent. Paper and crayons and pencils were strewn across the white tables. I spotted a picture of a black bicycle. It stood out from the sheep and the horses and the maybe spaceship. Colin must have thought so too, because he pinned the '1st prize' rosette on it. I counted ten pictures of horses. Colin gave second place to the one whose head was in proportion to its body. He gave third prize to a painting of a golden Labrador.

'I'm tempted to give highly commended to this one,' said Colin, pointing to a picture that was composed of a simple black squiggle.

'Maybe not,' I said.

'Jacki, this kid could be the next Kandinsky.'

'I don't think it would go down too well with the parents,' I pointed out.

'Yeah, Mary would kill me.' He gave the last two rosettes to a painting of a little cottage and a collage of a bowl of fruit.

We sat down at the kiddie-sized tables and I started to doodle on one of the blank pages with a crayon. The tent began to fill up with little kids. Most of them were too young to even understand the concept of a competition. One child came over to the table and started to chew on a crayon. I hoped he wasn't going to choke on it.

Suddenly a little girl's scream echoed through the tent. 'Maaaaam! I got FIRST!'

'You've got a great little artist there,' said Colin to her mother.

The little girl had light blonde hair that fell down her back and when she turned round to face her mother, with her finger still pointing straight at the rosette, I recognized her immediately.

> *Miss Jane had a bag*
> *And a mouse was in it.*
> *She opened the bag;*
> *He was out in a minute.*

We headed back out to the stage to catch the result of the pageant. Sarah had won. Her acceptance speech was short and not too boring; she must have rehearsed it, yet she made it seem as if she was so shocked to win. Shortly afterwards Rita phoned me to tell me I'd won the doll! I was delighted – it's always exciting to win something. By six o'clock the stalls were packing up, and everyone was getting ready for the performance by the Avarna Céilí Band. Colin had persuaded Emily to go on the carousel with him and I sat on the steps of the funhouse. I held the doll in my hands. The name Jane seemed to suit her. I used to find porcelain dolls a little creepy when I was younger . . . the way their eyes stared . . . But this one felt different. She had gentle green eyes, black hair and wore a pretty peach dress.

It began to drizzle, so I put the doll into my patchwork bag and went inside to shelter.

Typical funfair music played in the background as I walked around inside the funhouse. I seemed to be the only person there. There was no sound except for the music. It looped over and over, the whole thing consisting of just eight bars. It wrecked my head. The funhouse was divided into rooms, and you moved from one to the next through circular doorways. The first room was full of distorted mirrors. In the first mirror I was tall and leggy, towering over my actual self, and in the second mirror I was twice my width and half my height, my head crushed down into my body, so I had no neck. And in the next one half my face bulged out, as if a giant bump had swelled up on my forehead. I wished Colin was with me; we would have had a great laugh.

The next room was a pit of multicoloured balls, and I had to drag my feet through them to get out. In the room after that there were different-coloured revolving circles on the floor. The funhouse was quite dark, the walls illuminated by twinkling gold lights. It had an eerie quality and I wondered if Jane would appear. It was dark and claustrophobic, like the forest and the back of the café. It made sense that she'd pick here. If she came back, I'd try to get a closer look at her . . . find out what she looked like. Maybe this was what she wanted . . . Maybe this was where I was supposed to end up. I took a step back and whispered. 'I'm listening.'

A loud voice startled me. It was coming from outside. It was a man, yelling and cursing angrily.

'I can't believe you did that!' The voice was familiar. I realized it was Des. A sliver of light snuck in through a gap in the back wall. I bent down and peeked through it. Des was standing beside the generator, next to Chris.

'I didn't mean to!' said Chris, his voice shaking. Chris bent down and started to wind up a length of wire, but Des snatched it from him.

'Just leave it alone. Leave the wires. And turn that switch off!' Des was frighteningly angry. I'd never heard him raise his voice. I watched him inspect the generator while Chris shuffled about awkwardly. It was frightening to hear such venom and anger in his voice – it seemed so out of character. Des gave Chris a dirty look and then stormed off.

I rushed out of the funhouse and ran over to the carousel. I didn't want Des to see me. I didn't want to have to talk to him. Maybe there was a darker side to his personality after all. And, if he had killed Beth, then maybe he had killed again. Maybe he had killed Jane.

Chapter 19

The next day Mum was standing in the front garden in a gypsy dress and cardigan, her pink sling-back sandals hidden in the long grass. She was looking up at the house. The weather was getting cooler, the summer slipping away steadily. I was wearing my faded skinny jeans, a white T-shirt and grey waistcoat, each of its buttons encrusted with a little jewel. I stepped out of the caravan and walked across the grass. Mum didn't budge; she just stood there, staring at the house. She'd been so upset when I'd told her about Des. At first she didn't believe it, but then she'd found out that quite a few people in the village suspected him, so she'd decided to cool things off. She hadn't spoken to him for a few days. I didn't want to tell her about his angry outburst at the fête. It would only upset her more.

'Are you all right, Mum?' I asked, touching her arm.

'Hmm?' she said, looking at me. It was sad to see her like this. She'd really been into Des. I wanted the old Mum back. The one who flicked ferociously through home magazines for decorating ideas and got overly excited when kitchen units and bathroom tiles arrived.

'Are you OK?' I said.

'Yes. Yes, I'm fine. I was just thinking . . .' Mum shuffled her feet in the grass.

'About what?'

'Nothing important really . . . you know, just . . . stuff. The house looks great, doesn't it?'

'It's beautiful,' I agreed.

'It's exactly how I imagined it would be,' she said, her words positive, but her tone deflated. I knew what she was thinking about. Or, rather, who she was thinking about. I wanted to say something comforting, something to make her feel better, but I just couldn't think of anything. She probably didn't want to talk about it anyway. I knew that's how I'd felt, when I'd had my heart broken. I didn't want to talk about it, because it hurt too much. I thought it best just to stand there in silence. It wasn't awkward with Mum; it was nice. We didn't have to talk; we could just be. She knew I felt bad for her, she knew I cared. It was kind of overwhelming when I thought about all the millions of reasons why people broke up. There were so many obstacles, so many things that could go wrong.

Suddenly, we heard a loud noise like falling stones behind the house. The sound startled me. The builders weren't here. I wondered what it could be. I turned to Mum.

'What was that?' I said.

'Sounds like something fell,' said Mum. 'I hope nothing's damaged.'

We hurried round the back.

'Maybe it was a cat or something,' said Mum as we turned the corner. We looked around the garden. The stack of red bricks in the corner had been knocked down and strewn across the ground. But it wasn't a cat. We just caught a glimpse of a man disappearing through a gap in the hedge.

'Who the hell was that?' said Mum.

I was afraid to say who I thought it was.

'That looked a bit like Des,' said Mum. 'Did you see his face?'

'No, I didn't see his face, but it could have been him.' I was getting worried now.

'Why would Des climb through our hedge?' Mum sounded more confused than frightened.

'I don't know . . . but I have a bad feeling about him.'

'What do you mean?'

'Mum, I'm not sure he's that innocent any more. I overheard him get really angry with someone at the fête. Maybe he's not as nice as we think he is.' I didn't want to upset her, but I had to be honest.

'Hold on . . . could he have been spying on us?' Mum looked worried now.

'I don't know. Maybe –'

'That's it. We're leaving.'

'Mum, calm down.'

'Jacki, I can't deal with this any more. He was spying on us. A lot of people think he killed a woman. We need to get out of here. C'mon, let's pack up.'

'But –'

Mum marched towards the caravan. All I could do was follow her. She pulled her suitcase out from under her bed and began to fling things into it.

'Mum, can we talk more about –'

'Now!'

'Mum –'

'Put some things in a bag. We're going back to Dublin.'

'Dublin? No! We can't go back. I need to be here.'

'You can still see that Reynolds boy.'

'It's not only about him. I need to be here, Mum.'

'We're not coming back until the house is finished. I'm not staying in this caravan.'

This wasn't fair. I couldn't leave now. Jane needed me. I could cope with not seeing Nick, but I couldn't cope with letting Jane down. I went into the bathroom, pretending to pack up my make-up, but really just trying to figure out how I was going to stall Mum. When I came back out she looked terrible. Her hands were shaking and her face was white with shock. I watched her put some freshly washed clothes into her suitcase along with her make-up and jewellery.

'Mum –'

'Jacki, pack your stuff. Now!'

'I don't want to go –'

'This is not up for discussion. And we're going to the Garda station first. I'm not letting him get away with that sort of thing.' Mum was really mad. I could tell there was no use trying to reason with her when she was in this state. I'd wait until later. Maybe after driving for a while she'd calm down, and I'd be able to convince her to come back. I didn't want to leave Avarna now. Not even for a day.

I grudgingly piled my clothes and shoes into my own suitcase, scurried around looking for my notebook, then stuffed it into my handbag along with my phone and my iPod. Mum ran outside, opened the boot of the car and threw her suitcase in. I followed her out and put my suitcase on top of hers.

'Right. Ready?'

'No. Wait two seconds. I have to get my guitar.' I had to bring it, just in case this was for real and we had to leave.

Mum drove down to the Garda station.

'Can I go to Colin's?' I asked. 'He said I could stay over whenever I wanted. I could keep an eye on the house until you come back.' I knew it was unlikely she'd let me, but it was worth a shot.

'Are you crazy, Jacki? I'm not leaving you here.'

'But he said it would be OK.'

'You're coming back to Dublin with me. We can stay with Gran for a while till the house is finished. Now wait here. I'll be back in a second.' She got out of the car and slammed the door shut.

'No, I'll come with you,' I said. I got out too and followed her to the station door. She didn't protest. I think she was probably glad that I was coming in with her; she still looked pretty shaken up.

The front part of the Reynolds's house functioned as Avarna's Garda station, while the back served as the family's living quarters. The station was painted dull cream and blue and the cabinets and furniture were well worn. Sergeant Michael Reynolds sat at his desk behind the counter, flicking through a pile of paper.

Mum put her elbows on the wooden counter and Michael looked up, not with a jump, but with a slow, composed lift of his head.

'Can I help you, ladies?'

'We have a problem,' said Mum.

Michael placed his mug of coffee down on the coaster.

'I'd like to report an intruder,' she continued. I saw tears starting to well up in her eyes, so I interrupted.

'We think someone might have been spying on us,' I said. I wasn't used to seeing Mum like this. She was always so together, so in control. I knew she'd be really embarrassed if she ended up crying in front of Sergeant Reynolds. I put my hand on her arm, trying to comfort her.

'Someone?' said Sergeant Reynolds. 'Do you have any idea who it might have been?'

I was about to say his name, but I didn't want to jump to conclusions, so I just shrugged. Sergeant Reynolds seemed to know I was holding something back.

'Any idea at all?' His intimidating stare was enough to make me cave.

'Well . . .' I said. 'The guy did look a bit like Des . . .'

'Des Butler? Isn't he working on your house?' Michael said with a snort.

'He's finished working on it,' said Mum. 'I'm a bit worried . . . because we went out together a few times, you see, but then I heard a rumour about him, so I decided to stop seeing him. I think he might be . . . well, stalking me.'

'When did this happen?' said Michael, suddenly much more interested in what Mum had to say. 'You think he intruded on your property?'

'About twenty minutes ago. I think he was watching us from round the back. This whole thing is stressing me out. I think Jacki and I should go back to Dublin for a week or two until the house is ready.'

A week or two? No, I couldn't do that. I had to stay here. The door of the station swung open and Peter Mulvey popped his head in. He was wearing a black suit with a white shirt, the collar unbuttoned.

'Michael, are you free later for a round of golf?' he said before he had even stepped inside. Then he saw us and nodded in our direction. 'Hello, ladies,' he said. 'Sorry for interrupting.'

'Don't be trailing mud into my station,' said Michael, pointing at Peter's mucky shoes. Peter wiped his feet on the mat and pushed his sunglasses up on to his head. 'Ah, will you calm down, Michael,' he said. 'And what are a beautiful pair like ye doing hanging out in this dump?' He walked over and stood between the two of us.

'We're having a bit of trouble,' said Mum. 'We've had an intruder . . .'

'Oh dear,' said Peter.

'No prizes for guessing who,' said Michael, rolling his eyes. Peter gave him a knowing nod. Almost everyone seemed to have suspicions about Des. I still couldn't believe nobody had told us. Michael wasn't doing much to curb Mum's fears.

This meant that I might actually have to accept that I couldn't stay in Avarna. It was so unfair.

'We're going back to Dublin,' added Mum. 'I won't feel safe until the house is finished.'

'Now don't be too rash. You're very welcome to stay at our house,' said Peter. 'You'll be safe there. We have electric gates, CCTV, an alarm system –'

'Really?' I said. This might be a good solution. The Mulveys' house was huge . . . Mum and I could both stay there. I was glad Peter had come into the station.

'Thanks, but we don't want to burden you,' said Mum. 'We should go back to Dublin. We can stay with my mother for a week or two.'

I should have known Mum wouldn't accept. She'd always

been reluctant to accept help from people, especially people she didn't know well. She was used to sorting everything out herself, used to being totally independent.

'But you're trying to finish your house, aren't you?' said Peter. 'You won't be able to do that if you're back in Dublin. And you wouldn't be a burden. I'm sure Anne won't mind. We have three spare rooms. You've met my wife, Anne, haven't you?'

'Yes,' said Mum. 'But really I –'

'I think it would be a good idea for you to stay at the Mulveys',' said Michael. 'And neither of you go walking around the mines or the forest by yourselves. We all know what that man is capable of.'

Mum looked frightened. Peter placed his hand gently on her back.

'Come on,' he said. 'You're in no fit state to drive anywhere, let alone Dublin. Come on back to my house and I'll make you a cup of tea. And you can think about my offer.'

Please say yes, I thought. *Please, please say yes.*

'OK,' said Mum, trying to compose herself. 'Thanks very much, Peter.'

I couldn't believe it. She was actually considering taking his help. Maybe it was because Sergeant Reynolds had advised her to. Or maybe it was because the stress of everything had just become too much. I didn't really care what the reason was though. All I cared about was that I might get to stay.

Chapter 20

Anne Mulvey placed a mug on the table in front of Mum. Mum smiled and took a sip. After twenty minutes of convincing, Mum had decided to take Peter up on his offer. I was so relieved. Now I sat at the Mulveys' kitchen table, buttering my slice of toast.

'Are you sure you wouldn't like a cappuccino, Jacki?' asked Anne.

'No, thanks, tea's fine,' I replied. The modern kitchen screamed expensive, but it had a lived-in feel, with a stack of dishes beside the sink and a pile of dirt beside the dustbin, still waiting to be swept up and disposed of. It certainly was a lot tidier than it had been at the party the week before, when empty beer cans had covered the counter.

'You're sure it's OK, Anne?' said Mum.

'Of course! What's the point in having three guest bedrooms if we never have guests? You can stay as long as you like.'

Anne Mulvey was a tall, thin woman with a spray-tan and a blonde hairstyle that was a bit too long for her age. Her hands were showing the first signs of wrinkles, but her forehead was impeccably smooth, suggesting she got something pumped into it. Her clothes were perfectly fitted and her shoes were the kind any self-respecting fashionista would kill for with her bare hands.

'Well, it will just be until our house is finished.'

'It's terrible what you have to put up with. That man should have been locked up years ago. Honestly, it's beyond belief.'

'Where's Dad gone?' said Carla from across the table. She was wearing the same outfit she'd worn to Emily's: a black hoodie with a red cross on the front, a short black tutu-style skirt and black Converse trainers.

'He's in the office, darling. He's closing off a very important deal tomorrow, so he'll be working late.'

'Well, could you remind him to leave my allowance here? I'm going to watch TV in my room.'

David sat at the breakfast bar in the middle of the kitchen, watching videos on his laptop. He beckoned me over. I sat on the stool beside him, my toast in my hand.

'Check this out,' he said, pointing to the video of a skate-boarding dog.

'Aww, that's so cute,' I said.

'Wait till I tell the guys you're staying here,' said David. 'They're going to be ragin'. Here, pose for a picture with me.'

David put his arm round me and the computer's camera clicked.

'Somebody has a new profile picture!' he said with a grin.

'Did you see the picture of Nick kissing that skanky girl?' I said.

'What girl?'

I logged into my account and found the picture.

David looked at it closely. 'That's not Nick.'

'Yes, it is,' I said. 'That's his hoodie.'

'That is definitely not Nick. That guy is drinking cider. Nick never drinks cider. And I don't think he was wearing that hoodie at the gig. That's not him, Jacki.'

I couldn't believe it. This changed everything. So this wasn't a photo from the night he went to Sligo. I had jumped to the wrong conclusion and now I had no reason to hate Nick. Not that I'd ever really let myself hate him . . .

'You're sure?' I said.

'I'm positive,' said David, closing the window. 'Ooh, my album is downloaded. Wait . . . what the hell . . .'

'What?'

'Look at this . . .'

'Oh my God . . .'

'Mum!'

'Yes, David?'

'Look what Carla has been looking up.'

Anne walked over to David, put her hand on his shoulder and peered at the screen. She jumped with shock when she saw the picture.

'Oh my God . . .'

'*How to slit your wrists*. She must have deleted the search history because it's empty, but she forgot to delete this picture from the downloads.'

Peter came into the room. 'Time for a coffee break,' he announced.

'Dad come here and see what Carla has been looking at,' said David, turning the computer towards his father. He maximized the picture of the hand, blood dripping from the slit cut into the wrist and staining the fingers.

Peter took one look at the stomach-turning image and then shouted 'Carla!' so loudly that it hurt my ears.

'What!' she said, coming back into the kitchen. 'Do you have to *shout* like that?'

'Explain to me what this is,' fumed Peter, pointing at the computer screen.

Mum and I looked at each other. Both of us felt uncomfortable about being here for such a personal conversation, but felt kind of trapped.

'Gross. Why are you showing me this?'

'Your brother found it on the computer,' Anne interjected sharply. 'And it's nothing to do with either of us.'

'Well, that goes for me too. You know I hate the sight of blood.'

'Carla,' said Peter, clearly calming down. 'If there's something wrong –'

'Dad, I swear it wasn't me. I swear!' shouted Carla.

'Well, it wasn't David, and it certainly wasn't your mother!'

'It wasn't me!' she said, and stormed off, slamming the kitchen door behind her.

'Sorry you had to see that,' said Anne. 'We've been having some problems with Carla lately. Perhaps we should make an appointment for her to see someone, Peter?'

'Yes,' said Peter. 'Maybe we should.'

I lay on the very comfy bed in the spare bedroom at the end of the hall, trying my best to get the image of the slit wrist out of my head. I couldn't believe that Carla was contemplating doing that. Maybe she was just curious to see what it looked like. I had presumed the grungy clothing and heavy eye make-up were just a fashion statement, not an expression of her inner feelings. I really hoped she wasn't planning on doing herself any harm.

A beautiful lamp stood on the bedside table to my right. It had a cream base with a blue butterfly design. Everything in the Mulveys' house seemed glitzy and expensive. I began to imagine that if I was as rich as the Mulveys I'd build my own recording studio in the house. It was fun just to lie there and fantasize about something silly for a change. I turned off the light and tried to sleep, but I kept thinking about Carla. I considered asking her if she was OK, but I didn't want to upset her. I didn't want to upset any of the Mulveys. They were the one reason I was still in Avarna and not on my gran's couch in Dublin. I needed to be in Avarna. I needed to help Jane. And I needed to fix things with Nick. I knew my chances were slim, but that didn't stop me formulating a plan to get him back. How would I explain what had happened to me at the party? How would I convince him I wasn't crazy?

I took my notebook out from my patchwork bag and put it inside the white bedside locker. I wanted to keep it safe. Safe like Mum and I were now, under the solid roof of a house with an electric gate, CCTV and an alarm system.

Chapter 21

The next morning I put on my Joy Division T-shirt, denim cut-offs and pink Converse, and unpacked the rest of the stuff from my suitcase. I figured we were going to be here for at least a week, so I might as well unpack everything. The house was supposed to be finished in a week, but it had been delayed before, so I didn't want to get my hopes up. I put my clothes in the wardrobe and the rest of my things in the bedside locker. Then I saw that Mum had put a note under my door – she had gone to the big hardware store in Carrick. David's door was closed. Downstairs, Anne was reading the paper in the kitchen.

'Help yourself to some cereal,' she said with a smile.

I ate quickly and told her I was going to meet a friend. I unwound my earphones and headed straight for the village. The air was sticky with heat, but a huge grey cloud threatened rain. As I passed Nick's house I turned up the volume on my iPod to distract myself from the pain in my chest that came whenever I thought about him. I wondered if he was in there, but I couldn't bear to face him. Not yet, not until I'd figured out a way to fix things. I dreaded having to see him at Mary's party, but at least I wouldn't have to stay for long. I'd just go, sing my song and leave.

I went to the Cupcake Café to use a computer. Colin and Emily and the others were busy with work and family stuff, but I didn't mind. I wanted some time to myself. I treated myself to a strawberry smoothie and enjoyed a quiet hour chatting online to some of my Dublin friends, then I decided to go for a walk. I needed to think about Jane. I knew the clues had to be connected somehow. Mum had made me promise not to go anywhere near the forest or the mines, so I was confined to the village. I went down to the communal garden, but there were lots of kids there enjoying the last of their summer holidays. I scrolled through the music on my iPod, put on some Thin Lizzy and just walked around the village.

My mind kept wandering back to Nick. Everything on my route reminded me: Clancy's pub, the garden and of course the shop, which I couldn't even bear to look at. Part of me wished that Nick *had* been with some other girl. Then I might have had some chance of forgetting him. I wouldn't be thinking about him every second of the day. Now it was even harder than before. There was so much damage to repair – the major freak-out and the fact that I'd completely ignored him for a whole week. I hoped I'd get a chance to fix things. I took my phone from my pocket and checked the screen. There was no coverage. Typical. I really needed to talk to Hannah. She was an expert on boy problems – she'd know what to do.

And, as if I didn't have enough to worry about, I had absolutely nothing to wear to Mary's party. I hadn't packed any fancy clothes and had already worn everything in my suitcase about ten times. I was in desperate need of some company, so I headed for Lydia's shop.

I flopped down on the stool in Lydia's workshop. It was the messiest I'd ever seen it. I wondered how she was able to work in such chaos, but it didn't seem to bother her. She finished steaming a lilac dress, then turned to me.

'Right,' she said, 'my next project is a midnight blue bubble dress. So, The Clash or Bowie?' Lydia held one CD in each hand.

I wasn't really paying attention.

'Well . . .?' she said.

'Sorry, I'm a bit distracted.'

'What's up?' she asked.

'Everything. I'm supposed to help someone and I'm doing a terrible job, the guy I like hates me and I have nothing to wear to Mary's party tonight. Mum was supposed to bring me shopping but she didn't have time.'

'Well,' said Lydia, putting down the CDs, 'I can only help you with one of those things. But luckily it happens to be the most important one.'

'Thanks, Lydia, but I can't really afford one of your dresses. I'll just –'

'You can borrow one,' said Lydia. She bounced out of the workshop and weaved through the racks.

'Oh . . . no, it's OK.'

'Jacki, we're friends, right? Friends borrow each other's clothes. Now stop whining and pick something out!'

I smiled for the first time all day. 'Wow, are you sure? Thanks, you're a life-saver.' I liked that I could just be myself with Lydia. The big age difference didn't seem to matter.

'I think this short black one would look gorgeous on you,' said Lydia, taking it off the rack.

'I suppose I could have borrowed something of Carla's,' I said. 'But we're not really the same size.'

'Carla Mulvey? I didn't realize you were close with her.'

'I'm not really. But we're staying in the Mulveys' house.'

'How come? Is there something up?' she asked.

She slipped the black dress off the beaded hanger and gave it to me.

'Mum is worried about Des. She's a little bit scared of him ever since she found out he was a suspect in Beth Cullen's murder.'

'I don't think it's Des she should be worried about,' said Lydia.

'What do you mean?' I said.

'Nothing . . . I just have a feeling that Des didn't kill Beth. I don't think Rachel should be worried about him.'

'How can you be sure?' I said, unbuttoning the back of the dress.

'Trust me. I'm sure,' said Lydia.

'But how?'

'I just know he didn't do it.'

Lydia showed me the zip in the side of the dress. I stepped behind the folding screen and took off my T-shirt and shorts.

'Do you have any idea who did it?' I said, putting the black dress on over my head.

'Not a clue,' said Lydia.

'You know how you talked with her the afternoon she went missing?' I said. 'Do you remember anything strange? Did she mention she was fighting with Des?' Standing behind the screen seemed to give me a false sense of courage. It was easier to ask Lydia these questions when I didn't have to see her face. I felt bad. It was probably upsetting for her to talk about Beth, but I needed more information to piece together.

'How do you know I talked with her? Where did you hear that? Did the Mulveys say something to you?'

'No. I just overheard you talking to Mary in the pub the other night . . . I heard you mention something about having a fight. Sorry, I didn't mean to eavesdrop. I was sitting nearby and I'd only just heard the story about Beth so I couldn't help listening . . .'

'We did have a fight, yes.'

I stepped out from behind the screen, adjusting the dress's straps.

'That looks gorgeous on you,' said Lydia, her voice sounded a little deflated now.

'Thanks,' I said, feeling guilty.

Lydia sat down on her chair. I knew she didn't want to talk about this, but time was running out. I needed to find out what had happened.

'Did you know a girl called Jane?' I asked. 'Do you remember . . . her name was on that note Colin found in the attic . . . and guess what . . .' I reached into my patchwork bag to show Lydia the porcelain doll.

'. . . it's a coincidence but I named this doll 'Jane' and then won her at the fête.'

I've never seen anyone look so shocked.

'Oh my goodness. I can't believe it. This looks exactly like Beth's doll,' she said, taking it from me. 'Where did you get it?'

'This was Beth's?'

'Yes, or one exactly the same. She called it Jane,' said Lydia, stroking the doll's black hair. This was Beth's favourite doll. She called her Jane because that was her birth name.'

'Birth name . . .?'

'Yes, she was adopted. She found out her real name when she was nine. She was rooting in her parents' room and came across the adoption papers.'

The clues started to slot together in my mind. Things started to make much more sense. Beth and Jane were the same person! I'd been right in thinking they were connected, but I'd never have guessed this. I could hardly believe it. It was a relief to know that there hadn't been two murders.

'She didn't tell anyone but me,' Lydia continued. 'Whenever we played games she'd use Jane as her make-believe name. She carried it on into her teens. Whenever we wrote notes in class to each other we'd use our play names. She'd use Jane and I'd use –'

'Audrey.'

'Yes. Audrey Hepburn was my idol. I'm sorry I didn't tell you that was my note you found. I just hate being reminded all the time . . . It's so hard for me to talk about her. I feel so guilty.'

'Because of your fight?'

'I didn't mean to fight with her, you know,' said Lydia. 'I was just upset. When Beth got a boyfriend she didn't hang around with me as much as she used to. Obviously, she had to spend time with her boyfriend, but I didn't take it very well. I was used to doing everything with her. We'd been best friends since we were babies. The Cullens used to live two doors down, where the café is now. But when Ali was born they moved to a bigger house up by the mines, but we still saw each other every day. We even took violin lessons together.

When Des came along, instead of hanging out with me every night, she'd just call to visit me one or two nights a week. And some weeks I wouldn't see her at all. I was jealous. Then one day, it was coming up to Christmas, Beth cycled down to my house and knocked on my door. She was just back from a trip to England with her parents, visiting relatives. She took out this little egg-shaped thing from her pocket, wrapped in tissue paper, and gave it to me. It was the porcelain egg. She'd brought it back from England for me.

'I asked her if she wanted to go to the cinema that night – there was a new movie out that I really wanted to see. But she said she couldn't, that she'd already made plans with Des. Then she asked me if I wanted to go Christmas shopping with her that day. She said she was going to cycle into Carrick to buy presents. I knew she was expecting me to say yes. I knew by the look on her face that she didn't expect any other answer. So I said no. I said I'd already made plans with my mam and there was no way I could go. We had a fight and she went to Carrick on her own. And that was the night she was murdered. I've never forgiven myself for that, Jacki. I've never forgiven myself.'

'You can't blame yourself, Lydia.'

'Oh, I blame myself for a lot more,' she said.

'What do you mean?'

'Nothing. Forget I said anything. I shouldn't even be talking to you about this.'

'You can tell me, Lydia. I won't tell a soul. I promise. Do you know something?'

'I . . .'

'What do you know?' I said, my heart beating faster, aware that I might finally get some answers.

'I know who killed Beth,' she said, holding back tears. 'Because . . . because he tried to kill me too.'

I wasn't expecting that. I was so shocked I had to sit down.

'I was sort of going out with him,' said Lydia. 'Even though he was meant to be with one of my friends. One day we drove up to the mines and he picked me a bunch of flowers and told me how pretty I was. And then he kissed me. I didn't want things to move that fast. But he didn't listen – he just pushed me down on the ground. And I started screaming, but I couldn't stop him. He was so strong. But then we heard something, someone out walking their dog probably, and he panicked, and he let go. Then he told me if I ever told anyone what happened he'd kill me. And my parents. I believed him, Jacki. I believed him. That's when I suddenly figured out what happened to Beth. I knew that Des couldn't have been the one who'd killed her. And I knew she would have got into a car with this person. I knew she would have trusted him. It all started to make sense. But I couldn't tell anyone. I've just blocked it out and kept it to myself all these years.'

'Who was it?' I said. My heart was beating so fast that it was almost unbearable.

'I can't tell you! Please don't make me sorry I told you this.' There was a harsh finality in her voice, but I couldn't let her stop now, not when I'd got this far.

'Is he from here?' I asked. 'Is he from the village?'

'Yes.'

'Lydia, who is it?'

'That's all I can tell you. I'm sorry.'

I was so frustrated. But at the same time I felt so sorry for her, so sorry for what she had gone through, what she was going through now. 'How can you deal with that?' I asked. 'How can you live in the same place as him?'

'I know it's not ideal, but I'd find it hard to cope anywhere else. I don't know if Colin has told you . . . but sometimes I get very down.'

Colin hadn't mentioned anything about Lydia having depression. But I still didn't understand how she could live so close to someone who'd threatened to murder her, and who she thought had murdered her best friend.

'I'm sorry, I can't tell you any more,' she said. 'This man . . . he's too well connected. He'll never get done for it.'

Chapter 22

I knocked on Des's front door. There was no answer. But his van was outside, so I waited. I glanced up and down the street, hoping nobody would see me. Mum would be very upset if she knew I was going to talk to Des, let alone visit him at his house. But I knew he wasn't a threat now. I believed Lydia. And I needed to hear Des's side of the story. I wondered if he would even talk to me. I stood there for a few more minutes and eventually he opened the door.

'Jacki. What are you doing here?' He didn't sound mad, just surprised.

'I need to talk to you,' I said, shuffling on the doorstep.

'OK so. C'mon in.' Des was unshaven and looked exhausted.

I stepped into the hallway.

'Come into the kitchen,' he said. 'Mam is dozing off in the sitting room.'

'How is she?'

'She's a lot better.'

'That's good.'

Des was looking at me suspiciously. I would have to get to the point.

'Why are you here, Jacki?'

'I wanted to ask you about something. Well, someone, actually. Beth Cullen.'

Des sighed. 'I know what you've heard. But it's not true. I didn't kill her.'

We sat down at the kitchen table.

'Can you tell me what happened? If you don't mind, of course.'

'No, I don't mind. Especially if it's going to put your mind at ease. It was a long time ago, Jacki. We were very young. She meant everything to me. Her dad, Jim, asked me why I didn't cry at the funeral. Why I hadn't cried once since I found out she was murdered. They saw it as an admission of guilt. The fact that I showed no emotion. Truth is I couldn't accept it. I couldn't accept she'd been taken away from me.

'I saw her that day, the day she was killed. She was in Carrick buying Christmas presents and I was doing a job in one of the shops. She came up for a minute to say hi to me. I went outside to her. All her shopping bags were in the basket of her bicycle. She told me she'd got me something, but I wasn't allowed to see it till Christmas Day. Those were the last words she said to me. Since we first started going out, I'd never been apart from her for more than a week. I missed her like crazy. I missed her so much. I wanted to cry. I really wanted to cry. But I just couldn't let myself. Because if I cried then it would all be real. If I cried, then I'd have to accept it. And I couldn't. I just couldn't.'

I felt terrible for Des. This was so upsetting to listen to.

'Do you have any idea who did it?' I said.

'No. None whatsoever. I kept replaying that day in my head, but I don't remember anything suspicious. The day they found her body was the worst day of my life. Michael Reynolds accused me from the outset. Because of that, a lot of people in this village think I killed her. "*You're going to hell for this, Des Butler.*" That's what he said to me. And he was right. My life has been a living hell for the past twenty-five years. The way some people look at me. The hate in their eyes, and the disgust and the fear. I would never have hurt Beth.'

Des sounded so sincere and looked so sad there was no way I couldn't believe him.

Then he looked up at me.

'Jacki, I really care about your mum.'

'I know you do,' I answered, and meant it. 'Des, were you up at the house yesterday . . . in the afternoon?'

'No, I wasn't. I've finished working there for the moment,' he said. 'Where was I . . . I had to take my mother to the chiropodist in Carrick. Why?'

'I just thought I saw you . . . it doesn't matter. I'd better go. Mum will probably be wondering where I am.'

'I wish everything could be finally cleared up,' Des said as he saw me to the door.

I wished for that too.

As I walked along the path towards the Mulveys' house I felt both relieved and confused. Relieved that Beth and Jane were the same person. It was Beth who I'd followed into the trees, Beth who I'd seen in the café. It all made sense now.

But I needed to find Beth's killer. Lydia had said it was someone who lived in the village. And I knew it wasn't Des.

I heard someone call my name.

'Jacki!' shouted Mary from the door of the Garda station.

'Hi, Mary,' I called back, but continued walking, not wanting to get caught chatting for ages.

'C'mon into the house till I give you a bit of birthday cake,' she said.

I sighed and crossed the road.

'Nick isn't here,' she said as I followed her round the side of the station. 'He's down minding the shop.'

My heart sank slightly. After avoiding him for so long this would have been a good excuse to talk to him.

'I didn't really want to get a cake,' said Mary. 'But Rosie really wanted to blow out the candles, so I had to give in.'

'Oh yeah, happy birthday, Mary,' I said. I'd actually forgotten it was Mary's special day. My mind was racing, trying to link together all the clues.

'I was out checking if Michael wanted to have a cup of tea with myself and Joe,' she said. 'But the lads said he's gone for a walk up in the forest.'

As I imagined Michael weaving through the conifers, I began to wonder if perhaps he was the person I was looking for. Lydia had said that the killer was too well connected. She'd also said that the man who'd tried to kill her had been going out with one of her friends. And I remembered during the fight in the shop Mary had said he didn't have an alibi for the night of the murder. Maybe Mary even suspected her own husband. He certainly was a bully. The more I thought about it, the more suspicious I became. It was hard to believe he was Nick's father.

'I really better get going, Mary,' I said, wanting to get back so I could jot all this down in my notebook.

'Don't be silly, c'mon in. It won't take a minute. You'd better hurry before Joe Clancy eats it all!'

I reluctantly followed Mary into the kitchen. I glanced into the sitting room, where Mary's daughter and her friend sat on the couch watching TV. The volume was so loud that they didn't even notice us come in.

'Are you having a nice birthday?' I asked, trying to appear normal, not wanting to show any signs that I suspected her husband might be a murderer.

'Ah yeah. It's been quiet so far. Michael is taking me out for a meal later.'

'Hi, Jacki,' said Joe, who was sitting at the kitchen table, drinking a cup of tea. 'How are you?'

'I'm grand, and yourself?'

'Ah sure, can't complain. I was just dropping Mary down her present. Don't want her to think I've forgotten about her,' he said, giving me a wink. 'I better head on now. The missus will be wondering where I am. I'll see ye later.'

'Right you are, Joe,' said Mary as he left the kitchen. She took a slice of cake out from a tin and started to wrap it in tinfoil.

'It's black forest gateau,' said Mary, 'Nick's favourite. Actually I better remember to keep him a piece!'

The more I heard his name, the worse I felt. I really hoped I'd be able to fix things.

'Did you get anything nice for your birthday?' I asked, trying to change the subject.

'Oh yes. Well, I got that beautiful painting from Colin.' She pointed over to the far wall, at the painting I'd admired in Colin's room the first time I'd met him.

'It's stunning,' I said.

'It's wonderful. There's something special about it. And Lydia said she's dropping down my present later. My sister got me a nice bracelet . . . and wait till you see what I got from Joe and Rita. I'll just go and get it.'

Mary hurried out of the kitchen. I looked around the room. Everything in its proper place, everything neat and tidy.

'Here it is!'

She opened up a gift box to reveal a silver watch.

'Oh, it's lovely!'

'Isn't it gorgeous? I needed a new watch. Joe must have remembered that. He's so thoughtful.' There was a glint in Mary's eye that I hadn't seen before.

Chapter 23

'SURPRISE!'

'Oh my God!' screamed Mary.

Everybody cheered. I stood on my tippy toes, trying to see over the crowd. I shuffled in behind Emily, so I could get a better look at Mary's face.

She looked completely shocked. She had just stepped into the parish hall, which Brigid and Joe had transformed into a sparkling wonderland complete with fairy lights, silver streamers and gold helium balloons.

'I'm going to kill you, Brigid Smyth!' said Mary as Brigid gave her a big hug.

'Don't blame me! It was all Joe's idea!' she said with a smile.

'No wonder you were trying to get me to wear this dress, Nick! I can't believe this! This is . . . this is wonderful!'

'You deserve it,' said Joe. 'And may I say you look lovely.'

She did indeed. Mary was wearing the red silk dress that Lydia had made her for her birthday. It showed off her curves. She'd had her hair blow-dried and was wearing high heels, which meant she now reached Michael's shoulder. She looked so petite and vulnerable beside this huge man. It was the first time I'd seen Michael out of his police uniform and he looked quite smart in a dark grey suit and blue tie, but he was smiling half-heartedly. He looked like someone incapable of happiness. Couldn't he at least pretend to enjoy himself?

'So you didn't have a clue, Mary?' said one of the other guests. There were so many people there.

'Not a notion! I can't believe it!' At least Mary was having fun. That's all that mattered.

I tried not to look at Nick. But I couldn't help myself. He was wearing a suit. I don't think I've ever seen anybody look that good in real life. And he was smiling too. Why couldn't he be in one of his grumpier moods? His warm smile made him even more attractive.

Everybody went up one by one to kiss Mary on the cheek. I was one of the last to greet her.

'Happy birthday, Mary!' I said.

'Oh, thanks, Jacki. Thanks for coming. I can't believe this! You didn't give anything away earlier! I should have guessed Joe was up to something.'

'I love your dress,' I said.

'Thank you. Lydia gave it to me for my birthday. Isn't it gorgeous? I wasn't going to wear it, thought it was a bit fancy for a restaurant, but Nick insisted. Now I know why! I wasn't going to a restaurant at all!'

It was nice to see Mary so happy. She really did deserve it.

'Happy birthday, Mary!' said David.

'Thanks!' she said.

David looked good too. He was wearing denims and a black shirt, which he'd spent ages choosing. Carla and I were ready half an hour before him. There had been talk between Peter and Anne about whether Carla should be grounded, but I was glad that they allowed her to go to the party in the end. And Carla seemed happy in her own way.

'Jacki,' said Joe, '. . . can I have a little word?'

'Of course. Talk to you later, Mary,' I said.

'Yes, talk to you later. Oh my God! I can't believe this! My very own surprise party!'

Joe beckoned me over to the side of the stage. The band had just launched into a rendition of 'Congratulations'.

'I'm going to call you up to sing. I'm not sure when it'll be yet. We've to wait till Mary is settled and has said hello to every-body and everything.' Joe looked anxious. I suppose as one of the chief organizers of this big occasion he wanted everything to go just right. The hall looked great, and everyone seemed to be having lots of fun already. I wasn't nervous at all. I was excited about performing. I'd really grown to love the song.

'That's grand, Joe. Relax. Everything is going great.' I smiled and he smiled back, but I don't think he was really listening to me, because he rushed off, still looking flustered.

Everybody from Avarna was in the parish hall that night. Well, almost everybody. Des wasn't there. I wished he was, just so he could see my mum. She was wearing one of Anne's blue designer dresses and looked absolutely stunning. I had an idea of how insanely expensive it was, but I didn't tell Mum. It had a high neckline and dipped down low at the back. She looked like the movie star she'd always dreamed of being. I don't think I've ever seen her look so beautiful . . . except maybe in her wedding photographs. I hadn't told Mum about my visit to Des. Not yet. I wanted to be one hundred per cent sure before I told her anything. I didn't want her heart to break all over again.

'Who's yer one in the black dress? She's a bit of all right,' said a familiar voice from behind me.

I turned to see Colin standing there, in a black suit and white shirt.

'You're not looking too bad yourself, Colin.'

'Yeah, I scrub up all right, don't I?' He looked really cute.

'Want to go sit down?' he said.

'Yes. I do. These heels are killing me already.' I'd brought some pumps in my bag, but I refused to surrender this early in the evening. Besides, the heels looked so nice that they were totally worth the pain.

'Have you got your song sorted?' asked Colin.

'Yep. "Have I Told You Lately", one of Mary's favourites apparently. Joe is going to call me up when I've to sing it.'

'Joe has gone to a lot of trouble. I know my mam and Lydia went to a lot of fuss, with the decorations and the food and all that. But he really went to town on the personal touches. Oh, and fair play to you for coming.' Colin smiled at me sympathetically. I'd almost forgotten about Nick. Almost.

'Well, I couldn't let Joe down. I hope this won't be too awkward.' I glanced over towards Nick.

'Ah, don't worry about Nick. He's busy mingling. His granny has him trapped over there at her table.'

I wished he would talk to me. Even just to say hello. I kept looking over, hoping that he'd catch my eye.

Joe got up on the stage.

'Good evening, ladies and gentlemen! Now don't worry, I'm not going to give a speech.' There was a laugh from the crowd. I think Joe had a reputation for giving speeches that went on forever. 'I'm just here to announce that we will now be having the first dance.' This was my cue to go up on stage. 'The song will be sung by the lovely Miss Jacki King. I would like to invite our birthday girl, Mary, and her husband, Michael, to the floor.'

As soon as the band started to play the intro to 'Have I Told You Lately', Mary let out a little squeal of joy. I started to sing.

Joe and Rita joined the Reynolds. Rita smiled at Joe, and he clasped her hand, and put his arm round her waist. Brigid took Pa by the hand, and led him on to the dance floor. He gave her a kiss, and they started to dance. Lydia and Colin followed. Then David and Emily, and then Anne and Carla, and more and more couples until eventually the dance floor was packed with people. I looked at them all embracing each other, dancing together, laughing and smiling. Then I took a deep breath and sang the chorus one last time.

There was a round of applause. I stepped away from the microphone, and walked down the steps. Joe came running over to me.

'That was beautiful, Jacki,' he said. 'Just beautiful. You're an absolute star.'

'Thanks, Joe. Thanks for asking me.'

'What are ya havin' to drink?'

'I'm OK. I think I'm just going to go home now. I hope you enjoy the rest of your night.'

'What did you say?' said Colin, coming over to join us. 'No way you're going home! Nick is stuck talking to all his relatives. You won't have to talk to him. Come and sit down. I saw them putting candles on the cake – you can't miss that.'

I smiled at Colin. He was so kind and tuned in to what I was going through.

I wasn't sure if I could bear to watch Nick any longer. But I also hoped he wouldn't avoid me forever. Maybe if I stayed, there'd be a chance we could at least talk. 'Sure . . . I'll stay for the birthday cake.'

'What will ya have then, Jacki?' asked Joe.

'She'll have a Coke,' said Colin as he guided me towards an empty table.

As we sat down I decided I had to confide some of my thoughts to Colin; he was the only person I could tell.

'Colin, there's something we have to talk about.'

'Does his name begin with N?'

'Well, actually, it's sort of got to do with him.' I lowered my voice. 'I have a strong suspicion about who Beth's killer might be.'

'Wow . . . go on.'

'I've been doing some investigating and I think that it's . . . it's Michael,' I said, glancing over in his direction.

Colin leaned back in his chair and laughed. 'What have you been putting in your Coke, Jacki? Are you crazy? Have you forgotten that he runs a police station? Not to mention that he's the father of one of our best friends? I get that he's scary and all, but he's not a murderer.'

'I know how it sounds, Colin. Believe me, I wouldn't say this if I didn't have good reason.'

Colin looked at me in disbelief.

'Thanks, Joe, cheers!' I said as Joe delivered our drinks. He smiled at us as he wandered back to the crowd. I turned back to Colin and lowered my voice.

'Were you aware that Michael –' I wasn't sure how to put this as I hadn't seen it, only overheard it – 'that he pushes Mary around?'

Colin's eyes widened.

'I've overheard them fighting. One day in the shop.'

'Well, all couples have rows . . .'

'I know what I heard, and it wasn't just talking. But that's not all. I heard something else that makes me almost certain he did it.'

'What?'

'I can't talk about it here,' I said.

'Come on, Jacki, tell me.'

I couldn't tell him about my conversation with Lydia.

'What I can tell you is that he doesn't have an alibi for the night of the murder.'

'How do you know that?'

'Mary said it . . . when they were having the row I overheard.'

'Really?' Colin looked less sceptical now. Maybe he was starting to come round. 'I hope it's not true. Mary would be devastated.'

'And Nick.' It was a bit scary to think that the guy I really liked could be the son of a murderer, but I knew Nick wasn't anything like him. 'Thing is,' I said, 'I'm pretty sure it's true, but I've no way of proving it. Not yet.'

'Cake!' shouted Mary's daughter, Rosie.

Everyone stood up and sang 'Happy Birthday' to Mary, and watched as she blew out the candles and cut the cake. Joe took a picture of her with Michael, Nick and Rosie. They stood in a line with huge smiles on their faces, including Michael. Well, at least he was making a bit of an effort.

'Say *cheese*!' said Joe.

Soon the crowd started to chant 'Speech, speech, speech,' so Mary got up on to the stage and took the microphone.

'I would just like to thank everybody for coming here tonight,' she said. 'And especially all my relatives who travelled long distances, and my best friend Lydia Smyth for making me this dress.'

There was a huge round of applause and a few wolf whistles.

'Thank you to my husband, Michael, and my children, and to all my other friends, especially Brigid and Joe. I hope you all enjoy tonight.'

There was another round of applause and then Joe shouted, 'Time for the fifty kisses!'

'Are you going up to give Mary her kiss?' I asked Colin.

'I gave her one when she came in!' he said.

'I saw you gave her your painting.'

He nodded. 'Yes, I took it up to her house earlier.'

'She was delighted with it. I can't believe you gave it away!' It was such a beautiful painting. If it were mine, I probably wouldn't have given it away. But Colin was so talented that I was sure he could paint another one just like it.

'Well, I knew she'd appreciate it.'

'That was a really nice thing to do.'

'It felt like it didn't belong in my house anyway . . . that it belonged somewhere else. I'm not sure why. Art is like that, I guess.'

'Where's David?' I said. 'He was here earlier.'

'Yeah . . . I saw him go outside with Emily. I'm guessing they're all over each other out there. What's it like living in his house?'

'It's OK. I can't wait until we move into our new place though. I'm really looking forward to my own bedroom!'

'I can imagine. I can't help with that, but do you want some cake?' said Colin. 'Look at the queue. I'll go up and get us a slice.'

I watched him walk across the dance floor. The only people on it were a group of little kids, dancing to the band's songs, while everyone else was lining up to get a piece of the cake. Colin joined the back of the queue just behind Mum. I looked around at all the people seated at the tables, looking for people I recognized, and was surprised to see Ger Rapple. I hadn't expected him to be here but I was always surprised by how everybody seemed to know each other around here.

He caught my gaze and came over.

'Hi, Jacki,' he said. 'How are you?'

'I'm good, thanks.'

Ger was looking well. He was wearing a blue-striped shirt and a beige jacket.

'That was a lovely song. You're very talented.'

'Thank you!'

'How's it going . . . since we last met?' he said, a little quieter.

I couldn't wait to fill him in on all the developments.

'You're not going to believe this . . . Remember you told me about Jane –'

'Yes, of course.'

'Well, I found out that Jane *is* Beth Cullen. You know, that girl who was murdered in the forest twenty-five years ago.'

'Yes, I knew about that murder.'

'Beth is Jane. They're the same person.'

'Really? How's that?'

'Beth was adopted. Jane was her birth name.'

'Ah, that explains a certain amount.'

The little blonde girl from the fête danced past us, balancing a slice of cake on a paper plate.

'It's so weird,' I said. 'That little girl was singing a rhyme about Jane at the table quiz.'

'Very young children often connect with spirits,' said Ger. 'They're not frightened of them.'

That made sense, I guess.

'Have you any idea who killed Beth Cullen?' I said. 'I have a suspicion but I really need to find out for sure.'

'No, I've no idea who killed Beth,' said Ger. 'I once asked a fortune teller about it, but I didn't find out anything. Kathleen is a fortune teller I go to see in Dublin sometimes. I don't entertain many fortune tellers, but Kathleen is genuinely gifted.'

'What did she say?'

'She said the girl with two hearts will bring justice to Beth. God only knows what she meant by that. Beth will be waiting a long time for a girl with two hearts to show up,' said Ger with a laugh.

I turned to the side and pulled my hair back from my neck to reveal my freckle. Tiny and distinct. And in the shape of a heart. My *angel kiss*, as Gran called it.

By midnight there were still lots of people in the hall. The band was still going, and everyone sat round the tables talking and laughing. I was actually glad I'd stayed on. I hadn't really wanted to go back to the Mulveys' house by myself anyway; their alarm system was way too complicated. I decided to go outside for some air.

Joe was out the back, smoking.

'Hi, Joe. Great party!'

'Thanks, Jacki. Everyone seems to be enjoying themselves.'

I would have liked to talk to Joe about Mary and Michael. To find out if he knew about Michael's angry behaviour or about the alibi, but I didn't want to ruin the party for him.

Joe stubbed out his cigarette and went back in.

I stayed outside, staring up at the starry sky. Inside the band were playing a cover of Aslan's 'Crazy World'. The black dress Lydia had given me was the nicest thing I'd ever worn but I was getting a bit chilly. As I turned to go back inside I felt someone touch me on the shoulder.

'Nick!'

'Hi, Jacki.'

'Hi . . . I –'

'It's cool.'

'No, I want to explain –'

'It's OK. Colin told me that you were really stressed out about moving here and that it all got on top of you. I understand.'

Colin had made up an explanation for me. He was one of the best friends I'd ever had.

'Yeah,' I said. 'I didn't mean to freak out.'

'I know you probably thought I was . . . you know, being too pushy. But I . . . I just wanted to kiss you.'

'I didn't think that.' I took this escape route gratefully. I'd love to have been able to explain everything in detail but I wasn't ready for that.

'Have you been avoiding me?' he asked. I could hear the hurt in his voice.

I took a deep breath. Now was my chance to tell the truth. 'Nick, I'm really sorry. After that night I saw this picture that Emily posted online and I thought it was you kissing some girl. I . . . I thought maybe you'd found someone else. But it wasn't you, and even if it was I'd no right to think there was anything between us after what happened.'

He looked shocked. 'I haven't kissed anyone else. I haven't been able to think about anyone but you,' he said. He leaned over and kissed me on the cheek. 'I need to go. I have to take my little sister home. But we should do something soon, maybe the cinema or something. I'll text you.'

'Sure . . . cool.'

I actually could have cried with relief. There was hope.

When I went into the bathroom Mary was there. She seemed very happy. And very drunk.

'Jacki! Are you having a good time?' Her speech was slurred.

'Yes. A great time.' I was so glad I'd stayed. So happy that Nick and I had had a chance to talk.

'Oh, that's good. That's good. Your dress is lovely.'

'Thanks.'

I checked my reflection in the bathroom mirror. I reapplied my lipstick and fixed my hair while Mary washed her hands. Out of the corner of my eye I could see her looking at me. Like she was about to say something.

'Listen, Jacki . . . I know you heard me and Michael fighting in the shop the other day. It's so embarrassing, but . . . I'm sure it sounded much worse than it actually was.'

Mary's guard was down, otherwise she never would have mentioned anything about it. She was so drunk she probably wouldn't even remember this conversation in the morning. I wasn't going to miss the opportunity to find out more.

'I, em . . . I heard you say he didn't have an alibi for Beth's murder,' I said.

'Yes . . . I made one up,' said Mary, looking at me with glazed eyes. She lowered her voice to a hush. 'See, he was at a poker game. He had a bit of a gambling problem back then, and he didn't want any of the other Guards to know about it. They all thought he had given it up.'

'You're sure he was at this game?' I asked. I was surprised. If he was, then this changed everything. Maybe Mary was covering up for him? But was she capable of that in her state? Maybe she was so used to telling this lie that she had actually started to believe it.

'Sure, I picked him up from it. He had been there all night. He just didn't want to use it as an alibi. Why?' she asked, perhaps regretting that she'd said so much.

'Oh, nothing . . . I was just wondering. Enjoy the rest of your party!'

'Oh, I will,' said Mary as she turned back to the mirror.

I went into the cubicle and closed the door behind me. If Michael Reynolds's alibi was genuine and he didn't kill Beth Cullen, then who the hell did? Had Lydia and Des lied to me? Were they two of the best actors in the world?

'Hi, Mary!' said a familiar voice on the other side of the door.

'Hi, Rachel,' said Mary. 'How's the house going?'

'Great! The landscapers are coming in tomorrow. I will be glad to get that hedge cut down.'

I didn't realize Mum was having the hedge taken down. The leather bag was hidden in it! I needed to get it out of there before the morning. I'd have to hide it somewhere else. I slipped on my black pumps and decided to try to run back to the caravan before anyone noticed I was gone.

*

There was nobody else in sight as I turned off the main street and up our lane. I ran behind the caravan, rooted in the hedge and pulled out the bag. Then I unlocked the caravan door and stepped inside. There was a cold, unlived-in chill in the air. I dropped to my knees and rummaged under the bed. I pulled out Alf Meehan's letter, stuffed it in the bag and then looked through its contents again. A stick of lipstick, a packet of violin strings, a hat and a wallet. I opened the wallet, and searched through it again, but there was nothing in it.

Look in the bag, said that voice in my head. But I had looked in the bag. I had examined all its contents. There was nothing new.

Look in the bag.

I tipped it upside down, but nothing fell out.

I opened the two front pockets, but there was nothing in them.

I searched every inch of it. And that's when I found it. A zip on the inside, at the very back, hidden by the torn lining. I pulled the zip open. There was something in there. A card. I took it out.

It was a library card for the library in Carrick.

The name on it?

Elizabeth Cullen.

Oh my God. I knew this was important. I knew it was evidence. It would prove this was Beth's bag.

I put everything back in the bag and gripped the leather handles.

'Hello, Jacki.'

I recognized the voice immediately. I felt my insides collapsing with fear. I turned round, gripping the handles tighter.

Chapter 24

He was sitting in the darkness at the table. I hadn't heard him come in; he must have snuck in after me.

'Peter . . . What are you doing here?' I tried to act normal, even though my heart was pounding.

'Fancy yourself as a bit of a detective, do you?'

'What?' I said, trying to hide my terror.

He held up my notebook. How did he get that? He must have been rooting around in the spare room I was staying in. 'Nice little collection of clues you've got here,' he said.

I clutched the bag tightly. I remembered what Lydia had said. *He's too well connected.* She was right: Peter Mulvey was very well connected.

He lit up a cigarette. My eyes darted around the caravan. If I made a run for the door I'd never make it. If I screamed, it was unlikely that anyone would hear me. Everyone was down in the town hall. Everyone except me and Peter.

'I thought I ought to visit your back garden last week to have a little look . . . to see what had been dug up. But of course you and your mother interrupted me. I had to get out through the hedge before you could catch me. Scramble off like an animal.' Peter gave me a sick little wink. I suddenly remembered him trailing mud into the Garda station. The mud from our back garden.

'People already know about this,' I said. 'Even if . . . even if something happens to me. You won't get away with it.'

'All people know about are the delusions of a ditsy fifteen-year-old. With no evidence to back them up, they're hardly a threat to me,' he said with a laugh, flicking his cigarette ash on to the white plastic table. The tiny pieces of orange ash faded into black dust.

'And they definitely won't be a threat when you . . . when you're no longer here.'

I was terrified but I tried my best not to panic.

'You'll never get away with it,' I said. 'It's not like it was back then, you know. The forensics are way more advanced . . . you'll never –'

'You've been staying in my house, Jacki. My DNA will under-standably be on you. Besides I think we both know who is the more likely suspect. The man who has been stalking your mother . . . pestering you . . . The man who is already suspected of the murder of his own girlfriend.'

I tried to look unconvinced. 'Des wasn't stalking us.'

'That's not what your mother told Michael Reynolds.' Peter took another puff. 'Michael will know exactly who to blame when your body is found. But he'll never be able to even ask Des for a confession, will he? Shame.'

'What? What do you mean?'

'Well . . . I wouldn't be surprised if due to the guilt of killing you . . . Des hadn't tried to take his own life. Poor guy. He's probably lying in a pool of his own blood right now, his life draining away.'

He took off his glasses and wiped the lenses with his sleeve. I could see the evil in Peter's eyes. His pale blue eyes.

'No. You didn't . . .'

'It was actually pretty easy. Did you know Mrs Butler often forgets to lock their back door? Even though Des is constantly reminding her. Silly woman.'

'They'll know he didn't do it. If he dies, they'll know someone murdered him.'

'You know what, Jacki, the Internet is a very handy thing. Don't you think?'

I didn't answer. Peter took another puff of his cigarette as the realization hit me straight in the chest.

You have to move the blade in a certain direction. Don't cut the wrist at such an angle that the victim could not have comfortably done so themselves. You must cut before the victim is dead, as there will be no blood post-mortem. Be careful not to cut the tendons. Include hesitation marks. Be careful not to restrain the victim to such an extent that might leave bruising. Be sure levels of intoxication are not so high that the victim could not have inflicted the wound themselves . . . et cetera

I swallowed hard.

'Guess he just couldn't live with the guilt any longer,' said Peter with a smirk.

I felt sick inside. I needed to get out. It wasn't just my life I was fighting for. I was fighting for Des's too.

Peter flicked more ash on to the table. I bolted for the door.

He grabbed my hair before I could reach the handle. I dropped the bag as he yanked my head back and I fell on to the floor with a thud.

I kicked and screamed and scrambled back to the door, but he grabbed my wrists and held them above my head, and pressed his knees against my thighs to weigh me down.

'Feisty one, aren't you?' he said.

I suddenly realized I must have looked a lot like Beth Cullen, my hair plastered against my face and the brown leather bag lying by my side. It suddenly occurred to me that the vision in the master bedroom of the Mulveys might not have been about Beth Cullen. It could've been a premonition about me. After all, I'd been lying on Peter's bed.

'You have such a pretty voice,' said Peter. 'Pity nobody is going to hear it again. Now, this should shut you up,' he said, grabbing one of Mum's scarves to gag my mouth.

I don't know where I mustered the strength, but it came from somewhere. I head-butted him in the face, jumped up, kneed him hard in the crotch and with my free arm I grabbed the frying pan off the hob and bashed his head with it. He stumbled backwards and fell to the floor, hitting his head against the counter top on the way. I grabbed the bag and got out the door. I ran faster than I had ever done before. I ran for my life.

My pumps smacked against the tarmac. I could feel the sharp loose pebbles digging into their flimsy soles. But I didn't stop. I couldn't. I was so scared. I couldn't let anything happen to Des. My mum really liked him. And he didn't deserve this. He hadn't done anything. I ran past the bungalows, down the hill, then past the guesthouse and across the street. There was no time to go to the hall. I had to get to Des.

I fumbled with the handle of the front door for several precious seconds before pulling myself up over the little gate between Des's house and Mary's shop. I hoisted myself over its steel bars. My anklebones cracked as they hit the ground on the other side. I dropped the bag and ran over to the back door. It was locked. The sick bastard had locked it.

'*Hello! Hello!*' I banged my fist against the glass, and I kicked the wooden panels, but nobody came to open it.

'Hello! Open up! Open up!' It was pointless. The window. Get in through the window. It was locked too. But the glass was single glazed. I had no choice. I had to do it. It didn't hurt. I couldn't feel my fist slice through it. I couldn't feel the shards slitting my skin. I grabbed the handle, pushed the window open and climbed in. I clambered up the stairs and pushed his bedroom door open. That's when I saw him, slumped in the corner. His head hanging limply, his legs outstretched. Blood on his wrists. A Stanley knife lay on the ground.

'Des! Des!' He didn't look up. His eyes were closed; his body was still. '*Wake up! Wake up!*' His eyes opened for a second, but then they shut again. I ran into the hall and picked up the phone. I don't remember dialling the number, but I must have done. A voice answered immediately.

'What is your emergency?'

'I need an ambulance. An attempted murder. He's still alive but – OK. Number 16, Main Street, Avarna. OK. OK.'

I ran back into the bedroom, and knelt down beside him. I tore two strips from my dress, and wrapped them round his wrists. Des's face was getting paler. His eyes closed. I wasn't sure if they were ever going to open again.

Chapter 25

Peter Mulvey was tracked down at Belfast Airport just a few hours later, waiting for a flight to Frankfurt. He was arrested and taken to the Garda station in Carrick-on-Shannon. Des lay in a hospital bed in the intensive care ward, his situation critical.

Mum, shocked by the news, sat on her bed in the caravan, very concerned and utterly confused. I needed to explain everything to her. So I started at the beginning. I told her all about the headaches and the bag and the doctor and the healer and Peter Mulvey and how I had been wrong about Des.

'I always knew there was something special about you,' she said, brushing my hair back behind my ear and tracing her finger across my freckle.

I wasn't sure if you could call it special.

'So you're sure Des didn't kill anybody?' she said a few moments later.

'Yes. I am one hundred per cent sure. You can trust me on this one, Mum. Peter killed Beth. Des didn't kill anybody.'

'You said you had a bad feeling about him though?'

'I overheard him fighting with Chris at the fête, but Chris explained to me that he had overloaded one of the sockets at the funhouse. He was hungover and wasn't really paying attention. Des just got angry because one of the kids could have got hurt. He even apologized to Chris for shouting at him.'

'He's never going to forgive me . . .' she said, wiping tears from her cheeks. 'He spends half his life being blamed for a crime he didn't commit and then I come along and blame him too.'

'He will forgive you,' I said. 'He doesn't blame you. I know.'

Mum wanted to be by Des's side at the hospital, so I went with her. I never used to drink coffee, but I drank it that day, a sweet cappuccino from the machine in the waiting room that tasted disgusting. I think that in times of extreme emotion you notice everything more. I noticed the hot coffee on my tongue, the feel of the hard plastic chair against the back of my knees and the smell of disinfectant on the floors. I didn't like this heightened state. It reminded me too much of another day. That day six years ago when I'd watched my dad being buried. I tried not to let my mind go there. Des couldn't die. Mum would be so upset. I kept thinking maybe if I'd been able to run a little faster, if I'd left the party earlier, if I'd solved the clues in time, then it would have been different. And if I hadn't gone looking for answers in the first place Des wouldn't have got hurt.

Mum was allowed into the ward, but I had to wait outside. I didn't mind waiting. I liked it; I liked there being no news. I would have waited there forever, because that would mean he was definitely still alive. Every time Mum came down to check on me, I'd read her face for clues, and then feel a huge sense of relief when she'd say 'No change', and tell me to go home. After the fourth time that she told me to go, I went. I couldn't keep my eyes open any more. The adrenalin that had been keeping me awake was gone. I got a taxi back to the caravan. Colin was waiting by the door.

'I'm meant to be your sidekick!' he shouted. I took out my keys and walked towards him, too exhausted to shout back.

'You are,' I said.

He gave me a big hug.

'You didn't tell me about the Beth and Jane connection. You didn't tell me about Peter.' He looked so upset.

'I thought it was best to try to figure it out by myself. I'm sorry.'

'You could have died!'

'I'm sorry, Colin. I won't ever keep anything from you again.'

'Promise?'

'I promise.'

Colin slept in Mum's bed. I was so tired, yet I still found it hard to get to sleep. My mind was racing. And I kept checking my phone for news, even though I knew I had no coverage. I pulled the covers tightly around me, and eventually fell asleep to the sound of Colin's breathing.

The next morning there was no change. Des was still in a critical condition. I wondered what that meant. Was he more likely to die than to pull through? I asked Mum if she thought he was going to be OK. I'd needed her to say yes. I needed the reassurance that everything was going to be OK. But all she could say was, 'I don't know.'

That evening Mum, Colin and I drove to Carrick to hand in Beth's bag to the Gardai and make a statement. As I dropped it down on the counter I felt like a huge weight had been lifted from me. Like I was free. For now at least.

Chapter 26

One year later, on 2 November, Peter Mulvey was charged with the rape and murder of Elizabeth Cullen. Shortly after I'd handed the bag into the Garda station, Gardai had tracked down Alf Meehan in his new home and questioned him. He said that the bag did not belong to him and that Peter Mulvey had once asked him to burn it. Alf Meehan had suffered from a fear of fire all his life, and so, rather than burning it, he had buried it in his back garden, along with all his other unwanted rubbish. Before he buried it, he took the money out of it, but was not interested in the library card, or the violin strings, or the hat, or the lipstick.

When he heard of Beth Cullen's disappearance he had his suspicions. But he never said anything. Alf was a simple man, whom Peter Mulvey had a tight control over. Peter Mulvey was the only person who knew that it was Alf who had once stolen £25 from the church offertory. Peter was on a business trip when he heard that Alf was moving house. He sent him a threatening letter, just to make sure he didn't say a word to anyone.

There was much speculation regarding the exact events of the day that Beth Cullen went missing. The night I handed in the bag I had a dream. In that dream I saw exactly what had happened.

On the evening of 21 December 1986 Beth Cullen was cycling

home from Carrick-on-Shannon. That day she had bought Christmas presents for her parents and younger brother and sister and a packet of violin strings. She was about twenty minutes from her house in Avarna when Peter Mulvey pulled up beside her and asked her if she wanted a lift. Beth knew Peter well, from the ceili band and from the church choir, and it had just started to rain, so she accepted his offer. He put down the back seats and lifted her black bicycle into the boot. Beth sat in the passenger seat with her shopping bags and her brown leather handbag. A few minutes later Peter took a left turn off the main road that led them on to a much narrower one.

'I just have to drop something off to a man up here. Is that OK?' he said. Beth nodded.

'All set for Christmas?' asked Peter, his eyes glancing over at Beth as he spoke. She was wearing a blue dress that rested just above her knees.

'Almost,' she said with a smile.

The left front tyre hit a pothole hard.

'I better check that,' said Peter. He swerved into the right, to an opening in the forest and stopped abruptly. He got out of the car to examine the damaged tyre. Beth recognized where she was – they were parked near the mines, only ten minutes from her house. She opened the car door.

'It's stopped raining now,' she said. 'Mam will have the dinner ready. I could just cycle from here.'

Peter Mulvey stood up straight. And that's when she noticed his eyes. There was something strange about them. Something not right. He grabbed her arm and pulled her towards him. She screamed and kicked and desperately tried to pull away, but was helpless against Peter's brutal strength. He dragged her into the trees, pushed her to the ground and climbed on top of her.

'*Get off me!*' she screamed. '*Stop it! Get off me!*'

All the time he looked straight at her, looked right into her eyes with his own manic stare. She stopped screaming. He didn't like that. He wrapped his hands round her neck, and didn't let go until she couldn't breathe any more. He carried her body further into the forest and set it down on a carpet of twigs. Then he went back to his car, drove up near the church and dumped the black bicycle and the paper bags in the ditch. He ought to have gone home then. But he didn't. He drove back to the forest. He wanted to see her again. He wanted to see her face, feel her skin, kiss her lips. So he did.

As he drove back down the road, he noticed something under the passenger seat. A brown leather handbag. He had to get rid of it. He couldn't throw it out the window. He was too near the village. What if somebody saw him? He couldn't go back up to the mines. What if somebody was there? People might already be out searching for her. He knew who would take care of it. He swerved into Alf Meehan's driveway and ordered him to burn the bag.

I never dreamed about Beth Cullen again.

The search for Beth Cullen began on 21 December when her parents started to worry. They rang Des, who told them he hadn't heard from her since that afternoon. The bike and the shopping bags were found the next day but the body wasn't discovered until the 28th, one week after she was murdered. The body had been well preserved due to the very cold conditions. It had so many bruises. That's what Lily Cullen would always remember. So many bruises.

For twenty-five years Sergeant Michael Reynolds made Des Butler's life a living hell. Convinced that he had killed Beth, he dragged his name through the dirt, so that Des often found it difficult to get work close to home. He had no alibi for the night of 21 December so many people believed him to be guilty.

Following the discovery of Beth Cullen's body, blood samples were taken from approximately one hundred men living in Avarna and its surrounding areas. The blood samples, as well as the semen found on Beth's body, were preserved. Having been given new evidence in the form of the bag and its contents, after hearing my story and interviewing Alf Meehan, the Gardai decided to reopen the case. That day Sergeant Michael Reynolds requested a transfer from Avarna. He couldn't face the embarrassment that the man he had accused so publicly was actually innocent. He told Mary, Nick and Rosie that they were moving house. Mary refused to go. She stayed with her children in Avarna.

Why did Beth Cullen wait twenty-five years to get in touch? Because she wanted to wait until her father had passed on. She knew that if Jim found out that Peter Mulvey had killed her, he would have tried to kill Peter himself. So she waited until he had died, then she chose somebody to contact. She chose me.

I never received any official recognition from the Gardai. I didn't want it. I'd told them about my special ability, but I didn't want to publicize it. And I guess they didn't want it known publicly that crimes were being solved by fifteen-year-old girls who could communicate with spirits. I didn't hear from them again. Not until last night.

Epilogue

Still clutching the brown envelope, I dodged the puddles on the path that led through the grounds of Kilkenny Castle. I closed the top button on my trench coat and wandered along, taking in all the beauty of those noble surroundings. I'd gone for a walk to clear my head, to gather my thoughts and decide what to do. I had a choice. I could help with Operation Trail, or forget it existed.

I wasn't sure what to do, but I was almost certain that if I was to help Sergeant Lawlor I might have to go through the headaches and the nightmares all over again. But I couldn't exactly abandon those women in the photographs. They needed help, and I was one of the few people who could give it to them.

My head throbbed as I recalled what had happened in Avarna the previous summer. I wasn't sure if I could go through all that again. But maybe it would be easier this time around, now that I knew what to expect. I just wished somebody would decide for me.

The castle grounds were particularly beautiful that spring morning. The grass was damp with dew and the trees were pretty with their new leaves and small buds. I walked along, following the path, trying to reach a conclusion.

I sat down on one of the benches, opened the envelope and looked through the pictures again.

The first photograph was of a girl probably around my age. She had long red hair and was wearing a polka-dot cocktail dress.

The next girl had blonde hair like mine. She was sitting in the passenger seat of a car, with her bare feet up on the dashboard, looking into the back seat and smiling at whoever had taken the picture.

The third photo was of an older girl, maybe about 21, with short brown hair and a dimple on her left cheek. She was lying on a bed of grass with her hands above her head. She had beautiful blue eyes and thin red lips, and looked like she was in mid conversation.

The last picture was of a younger girl, with black hair and funky glasses. She wore an emerald green evening dress and was looking away from the camera, off to her right. Her hair fell in loose waves on her shoulders.

All young. All beautiful. All missing.

I put the pictures back in the envelope and kept walking along the path. I knew I had to decide soon. The more I thought about it, the more tempted I was to ring Sergeant Lawlor and tell him I didn't want to get involved. I didn't want to have those horrible headaches again. I didn't want to have nightmares every time I went to sleep. And I didn't want to put my life in danger. But maybe that was selfish. Maybe I had to put my own fears aside. Maybe I had to do this? I really didn't know what to do.

I noticed a striking sculpture to my left. It was tall and cylindrical, composed of lots of green metal hands, their fingertips reaching up to the sky. They were eerily lifelike, with realistic knuckles and fingernails. They looked as if they had been moulded from real people. I walked over to it, placing my hand on one of the metal ones. The sculpture was so unusual. I liked it, but wondered what it was supposed to represent. The hands were all touching, all joined together, yet they looked like they were reaching for something.

Come on, Jacki. You have to decide, I told myself.

'Dad,' I whispered, 'I know I can't talk to you. But you might be able to hear me anyway. I need you to help me. I need you to give me a sign.'

I turned round and walked back to the path. That's when I noticed the large stone facing the sculpture. It seemed to have some sort of inscription engraved on it. I moved closer and read:

This sculpture and area of reflection is dedicated to all missing persons. May all relatives and friends who visit find continuing strength and hope.

I had my answer.

Just as I reached for my phone, it started to ring.

'Hello,' I said.

'Morning!' Mum's voice was comforting as always. 'We're just leaving Avarna now, so we should be in Dublin around lunchtime.'

'I can't wait to see you!' I said. We'd arranged to spend a couple of nights in Dublin to visit Gran.

'How did your gig go?'

'It went great.' I hadn't decided whether to tell Mum about Sergeant Lawlor. But it definitely wasn't the kind of thing I could tell her over the phone.

'I'm sorry I missed it.'

'It's fine, Mum. Sure you've been to enough of them.'

'I know I have!'

'Tell her! Tell her!' I could hear Des shouting in the background.

'Tell me what?' I said.

'Well, we have some news.' She sounded a bit nervous. 'You're . . . you're going to be a big sister!'

'Oh my god . . . you're pregnant?' I was so shocked. But very excited.

'Yes!'

'Oh, wow! That's amazing! We can celebrate later!' I knew Mum and Des had been planning to have a baby, but I hadn't expected it to happen so soon. I was really happy for them.

'So we'll see you in Gran's?' said Mum.

'Definitely, I'm going to get the bus to Dublin soon. I'm meeting Hannah and the others for lunch, then I'll go straight to Gran's.'

'Great, see you later.'

'See you later!' shouted Des.

I had just hung up when the phone beeped with a text.

Miss you x

It was from Nick. I missed him too. Now I had so much news to tell him. But I had another call to make first.

I stood for a few minutes with the phone in my hand, staring at the screen. Then I took the white card out of my back pocket and dialled the number written on it. He answered straight away.

'Detective Sergeant Lawlor.'

'Hi,' I said. 'This is Jacki King.'

'Hello, Jacki. How are you?' He sounded very professional, but I could still sense the anticipation in his voice.

'I'm well, thanks. I've decided to do it. I've decided to help with Operation Trail.' As I said it, I could feel a familiar mix of fear and excitement rising inside me. This was it. There was no going back now.

'Thank you,' said Sergeant Lawlor. 'That's good news. I'll let the team know and will be in touch.'

I slipped my phone into my coat pocket, then turned and walked back towards the castle.

Four.

The number of women I have to help.

Acknowledgements

I'd like to thank:

My agent Faith O'Grady, my editor Paddy O'Doherty and everyone at Puffin for making my dreams come true. My first readers and researchers, especially Kitty, Charlene and Conal. Anthea, Liz, Martina and Laura for all their help and encouragement. My grandparents, godparents, aunts, uncles, cousins and friends for their enthusiasm. My beloved blog readers. Vanessa O'Loughlin for her support at every step and for being my literary angel. Sarah Webb, Claire Hennessy and David Maybury for giving such great advice and for welcoming me into their world. John Kilfeather for brightening up mine. My brother, Liam, for all his help and for always believing in me. And my parents, Joe and Jean, for everything.

GET INSIDE YOUR FAVOURITE BOOK

spinebreakers.co.uk

SPINE BREAKERS

spinebreaker (n)

story-surfer, word-lover, day-dreamer,
reader/ writer/ artist/ thinker